# Sugar Spinelli's Little Instruction Book

I knew there was something going on between those two youngsters years ago. Oh, yes. They thought nobody noticed them—but I don't miss much. Never did. Heck, you couldn't see the two of them on the same street and not spot the stars in their eyes. I thought for sure they'd end up in church. White lace. Flowers. The whole bit. Instead, they both up and left town.

Nobody'd seen either of them for years, until Ali came back and brought that little girl with her. Feisty little thing, but cute as can be. Looks a lot like I'd expect Jake Merrill's daughter to look. But I never said a word. Not one word. And I have a feeling Ali didn't either. I wonder what Jake's going to do when he finds out he's a papa....

Dear Reader,

We just knew you wouldn't want to miss the news event that has all of Wyoming abuzz! There's a herd of eligible bachelors on their way to Lightning Creek—and they're all for sale!

Cowboy, park ranger, rancher, P.I.—they all grew up at Lost Springs Ranch, and every one of these mavericks has his price, so long as the money's going to help keep Lost Springs afloat.

The auction is about to begin! Young and old, every woman in the state wants in on the action, so pony up some cash and join the fun. The man of your dreams might just be up for grabs!

Marsha Zinberg
Editorial Coordinator, HEART OF THE WEST

# Reclaiming
# Jake
# Patricia
# Keelyn

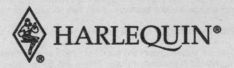

TORONTO • NEW YORK • LONDON
AMSTERDAM • PARIS • SYDNEY • HAMBURG
STOCKHOLM • ATHENS • TOKYO • MILAN • MADRID
PRAGUE • WARSAW • BUDAPEST • AUCKLAND

Patricia Keelyn is acknowledged as the author of this work.

ISBN 0-373-51157-4

RECLAIMING JAKE

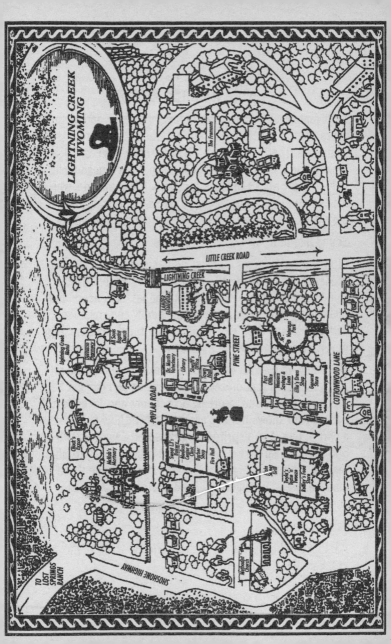

# A Note from the Author

Let's fantasize, for a moment. Close your eyes and picture yourself at an auction, where the items for sale are bachelors. That's right, *men*. All handsome, successful, and looking for Ms. Right. Okay, well, maybe that's pushing it, but *we* know what's in store for them. Now, imagine, you have the money to bid on one of these wonderful, sexy men. And you have a whole weekend to make him yours.

Sound like fun?

I thought so when my editor called and asked me to write the last book in the HEART OF THE WEST series. Then came the challenge—to take this wonderful concept and make it my own, to weave together family and romance with touches of the deep emotion that these relationships never fail to generate.

So I came up with Ali Kendrick, a woman on a mission to rid herself of her adolescent fantasies so she can get her life in order and start working on a family, and Jake Merrill, a loner who knows nothing about family or how to become a part of one. And a sprite of a girl named Sam, who will pull at your heartstrings even as she causes more trouble than an eleven-year-old girl should. How do these three manage to end up together? Read *Reclaiming Jake* and see.

Patricia Keelyn

P.S. I love to hear from my readers. Please write to me at P.O. Box 331, Hazelwood, NC 28738.

Thanks to Marsha Zinberg
for giving me a chance at another first.

And to Brenda Chin...again.

# CHAPTER ONE

ALI KENDRICK STEPPED OUT into the early Wyoming morning and shivered. By noon the temperature would climb to eighty, but for now, with the sun just peeking above the eastern horizon, she was grateful for her heavy flannel shirt. Wrapping her hands around a mug of steaming coffee, she leaned against the porch railing and drank in her surroundings.

When she'd moved to Lightning Creek two years ago, she'd bought this house because of its location. A mile north of town, the property sat on a hill overlooking the small Wyoming community. From her front porch Ali could see Main Street, its statue of a cowboy on a bucking bronc standing sentry over the traffic circle at the center of town, and the occasional glints of silver as the rising sun caught and reflected off the creek from which the town had taken its name. Closer in, the tall spire of All Souls Baptist Church rose above a grove of cottonwoods, whose leaves were still the fresh green of late spring. Farther away, she could just make out the bell tower of the Methodist Church. And in the distance, some fifty miles south, rose the Laramie Mountains, their eastern slopes rosy with the first blush of day, while the west lay slumbering in shadow.

Ali's property included a large rambling ranch house, several outbuildings, which had been easily converted into boarding kennels, and ten acres of good grazing land. For a woman who prided herself on her practicality and logical thinking, it had been the perfect choice for her fledgling veterinary practice. Falling in love with the view had been a bonus.

At the moment, however, she wasn't feeling very logical or practical.

She'd tossed and turned all night, both dreading and fantasizing about the day ahead. Two weeks ago she'd promised Lindsay Duncan, owner of the Lost Springs Ranch for Boys, that she'd attend and bid at the ranch's bachelor auction. Ali laughed silently as her stomach did nervous little flips. It had seemed like a good idea at the time, but now that the day had arrived, she couldn't bring herself to believe that buying a date with a man she hadn't seen in twelve years was a particularly sane decision.

Chester, her overgrown German shepherd, rubbed impatiently against her legs. With a soft laugh, she leaned down and scratched behind the big dog's ears. "You hungry, boy?"

Chester wagged his tail and looked at her with adoring brown eyes.

"Yeah, you and the rest of the crew." What foolishness, she thought, standing here daydreaming when she had work to do, animals to feed and tend. She'd made up her mind about the auction weeks ago, and she wasn't a woman to second-guess herself. "Okay, you shaggy mongrel. Let's go." With Chester close at her heels, she took her coffee and headed for the kennels.

It was no accident that Ali had ended up settling in Lightning Creek. She'd planned it from the time she was ten. After spending the summer here with her grandfather, she'd gone home to Atlanta and announced she wanted to move to Wyoming. To give her parents credit, they hadn't laughed at her outrageous request. Of course, they hadn't picked up and moved, either. Instead they'd sent her back every summer for the next eight years.

During her third summer, she'd met Doc Martin, who was the only vet this side of Casper. Ali had spent her vacation working in his kennels, and after that, not only did she know where she wanted to live, she knew what she wanted to do.

She loved the animals. Their nature and innate honesty appealed to some inner need of hers. Unlike people, they never lied or hid their feelings. No matter if they feared you or loved you, they showed it. Easing their suffering, whether it was something as simple as ridding a dog of fleas or as complicated as birthing a breech calf, left Ali with a sense of contentment. As if she'd done something good for the world. She never spoke about these feelings, figuring most people would think her idea of making the world better a little silly.

Usually, caring for her animals eased her mind and helped her forget her problems. But today she plodded through her chores, mindful of the passing time and the auction hovering at the end of her daily routine.

It was midmorning by the time Ali finished her work. She was heading inside to get showered and changed when a familiar Ford Bronco pulled into the yard. With Chester still at her heels, she changed direction to greet her friend. "You're early. This has *got* to be a first."

Gail Sebring climbed out of her car with a frown.

"You think you're the only person crazy enough to get up before the sun? Besides—" her frown turned to a grin "—with a man and three half-grown kids stomping around the house, I didn't have much choice."

Ali smiled, imagining the chaos at Gail's house. "So I take it John and the kids got off okay?" Gail's husband was taking their two sons and Ali's daughter, Samantha, hiking for the day.

"Bright and early. Just as planned." Gail squatted down to ruffle Chester's fur. "Hey, big boy. Who do you love?"

Chester let out a soft woof and licked her face.

Ali groaned. "That's so unsanitary."

"I'd hate to think of some of the things *you* do with animals." Chester rolled over onto his back, and Gail scratched his belly. "Besides, he's such a sweet boy. Aren't you?"

Ignoring the antics of the woman and the overgrown mutt, Ali asked, "Did Sam behave herself last night?"

"Sam always behaves herself. She's an angel."

"Hah!" Ali laughed abruptly. As much as she loved her daughter, *angel* wasn't the word she'd use to describe her rough-and-ready tomboy. *Hellion* would be closer to the truth.

"Well, she's always good for me," Gail claimed, as if reading Ali's mind.

"Some judge you are. You have two holy terrors for sons."

Gail grinned up at her. "And Sam fits right in."

Which was true enough. Sam and Paul, Gail's oldest, had been inseparable since the day they'd met. At first they'd squared off, circling each other like a couple of wolf cubs looking to establish dominance. Then the miraculous had happened. They'd decided to join forces, and heaven help everyone else. Lander Elementary would never be the same—to say nothing of their parents.

"One of these days," Ali said, "Sam's going to realize she's a girl."

Gail nodded sagely, as if contemplating the inevitable. "Paul, too." She stood, leaving Chester lying contentedly on the gravel driveway. "But hopefully neither will happen too soon. Meanwhile, stop worrying. John will take good care of Sam."

"It's John I'm worried about. With those three hell-raisers."

Gail laughed. "It'll be good for him. Give him a taste of what I put up with every day." Then, nodding toward the empty coffee mug in Ali's hand, she added, "Got any more of that?"

"Sure. Come on." Inside, Ali poured coffee for Gail, refreshed her own and started cleaning up the remains of her quick breakfast.

"So, are you excited?" Gail asked.

"Excited?" Ali turned toward her friend with a questioning look, though she knew exactly what Gail meant.

"About the auction."

"Oh, that." Nervous was more like it—terrified, even—but Ali couldn't admit either. Not even to Gail. Instead, she shrugged. "I guess."

"You guess? Gorgeous hunks parading on stage." Gail wiggled her eyebrows. "Having your pick..."

Ali laughed and returned to rinsing out the coffee-pot. "As if gorgeous hunks are something you're interested in."

"Hey, I'm married, not dead. So, what do you say? I hear some of these guys are pretty high-powered. A couple of executives. A lawyer. Even a doctor."

"I'm not interested in dating an executive. Or a doctor." *Or anyone else for that matter.* Which was why she needed to go through with this auction.

Gail arched an eyebrow and just looked at her.

"I think having a bachelor auction to raise money was a great idea," Ali continued. "And using the alumni was a stroke of genius. It would be a shame if Lindsay lost the ranch after all the good her family has done over the years. I'm just glad I can help out."

"Come on, Ali. You can't tell me you're not the least interested in the men."

"Actually, I feel a little foolish." Ali turned and, arms crossed, leaned against the counter. "I should have just written Lindsay a check."

"But that wouldn't have been nearly as much fun."

"The whole thing just kind of makes me feel…" She shrugged. "I don't know. Desperate." Which she was—in a way. Desperate to put the past behind her.

"That'll be the day. There are at least a half-dozen men in this town who would give anything for a chance with you. *You're* the one who's not interested."

Ali sighed, not wanting to get into a conversation they'd had countless times before. "Gail…"

"Don't worry." Gail held up her hands in defense. "I'm not going to bring up your reluctance to date again. Besides, I'm thrilled you decided to bid at the auction. As you said, it's for a good cause. Now, go on and get ready. We don't want to miss any of the action."

Ali wasn't so sure about that, but she pushed away from the counter, anyway. "Okay. I'll just be a few minutes."

Alone in her bedroom, she had no defense against the nerves coiling in her stomach. Gail had said the auction was all in fun. If only that were true. There was a lot more at stake than she realized. Ali's future, for one. And Samantha's.

She took her time in the shower, stalling and letting the water run cold before getting out. Then, annoyed with herself for taking so long, she quickly toweled off, dried her hair and applied makeup. When done, she pulled out a clean pair of jeans and a T-shirt but didn't put them on.

For the past twelve years she'd been piecing her life back together. It had been a long, hard road, but she'd almost made it. She'd finished college and veterinary school, moved to Lightning Creek, bought this place and set up her practice—all while raising her daughter. Now there was just one more thing standing in her way, one memory keeping her from moving on, keeping her and Sam from living a normal life. And today, Ali would take the first step to putting that memory behind her.

She shoved the jeans back in the drawer and went to her closet. A few minutes later, she returned to the kitchen. "Ready?"

Gail's face registered her surprise. "I didn't know you even owned a dress."

Ali laughed self-consciously. "Just because I never have a reason to wear a dress doesn't mean I don't own a few." She'd slipped on the simple summer sheath on a whim, but now she wasn't so sure it had been a good idea.

"You mean you don't like wearing dresses to stomp around some rancher's barnyard?" Gail crossed her arms and eyed Ali with mock amazement. "What's wrong with you, Ali? Where's your sense of style?"

"I left it behind when I entered vet school."

Gail considered that for a moment and nodded. "Makes sense. Somehow that pale peach wouldn't be the same with mud splattered all over it."

Ali laughed lightly. "It's supposed to get hot today, so I thought this would be cooler than jeans." Besides, she wanted to look good. Feminine. Then again, she wasn't about to admit that out loud.

"Plus, you're more likely to catch that doctor's eye."

Ali shook her head and grabbed her purse. Gail had come too close to the truth, though it wasn't a doctor that Ali wanted to impress. "Are you ready?"

Gail crossed her arms and frowned. "Is there something you're not telling me, Ali?"

A sliver of guilt slipped down Ali's spine. "No, why?"

"I don't know. You just seem…"

"I'm fine. Now, let's get going. You're the one who wanted to make sure we didn't miss anything." Besides, if they didn't get going soon, Ali figured she might just lose her nerve.

JAKE MERRILL GOT OUT of his truck and stood for a bit, transfixed.

Lost Springs Ranch. It had been twelve years since he'd last seen it, since he'd bummed a ride down to Glenrock, stuck out his thumb on I-25 and hitched his way with the first truck heading somewhere else. Yet it felt as if he'd never left. Despite the throngs of people for the auction, the place looked the same. Felt the same. He half expected Bob Duncan to saunter out onto the front porch of the main house and ask him where the hell he'd been *this* time.

Jake smiled to himself and pushed away from the truck.

Bob Duncan wasn't going to lecture him today. Jake would have gladly welcomed the rebuke, though, just to see the old coot again and apologize for the way he'd up and left all those years ago. And to thank him. Jake couldn't do either. Bob had died a couple of years ago, leaving the ranch to his daughter, Lindsay. So Jake was here because Lindsay had asked, and it was the least he could do for the daughter of the man who'd saved his life.

Jake started toward the house, half believing he'd run into one of the boys he used to hang out with. There were kids all over the place, but he didn't recognize any of them. This was a new generation of lost and troubled souls, and there was only one Duncan left to save them.

Besides the kids, Jake didn't think he'd ever seen so many women in one place in his life. They came in all ages and sizes, alone or in small groups. A pretty blonde in snug white jeans smiled an invitation, but he returned her smile without stopping. He spotted a reporter with a camerawoman and gave them a wide berth, as well. He'd had his fair share of dealing with the media, and it wasn't something he enjoyed. Tables had been set up under the trees to sell raffle tickets and a variety of homemade items, and country music blared from overhead speakers.

Lindsay had told him to check in with her or Rex

Trowbridge, the ranch's director, when he arrived, but the smell of barbecue drew Jake toward a large tented pavilion instead. It had been a long drive from Colorado, and he hadn't bothered stopping to eat. He'd find Lindsay or Rex later; there was still time before the auction got started.

Collecting a plate of food, he nodded toward a couple of guys who looked vaguely familiar, and started toward an empty table. He changed his mind when he saw a man in full military dress uniform sitting off to the side nursing a cup of coffee. Something about the guy tugged at Jake's memory.

"Nick?" he said, approaching the other man. "Nick Petrocelli?"

The man looked up, puzzled. "Yes?"

Jake set down his tray and held out his hand. "Jake Merrill." There was no way Nick was going to recognize him. Jake had been fifteen when Nick left the ranch to join the marines. "I was—"

"Sure, Jake. I remember." Nick took Jake's hand. "You were the kid who kept taking off into the hills."

"That's me." Motioning toward the empty seat across from Nick, he asked, "Mind if I join you?"

"Sure. Have a seat. You know," Nick added, stirring his coffee with a plastic straw and then pointing it at Jake, "I remember you about drove my aunt Karen crazy. She was never sure whether you were coming back or not."

"There was a time or two I wasn't sure myself." Sixteen years ago Jake had come to the ranch under protest, an angry thirteen-year-old with a chip on his shoulder and one last shot at avoiding Juvenile Hall. "Now, your uncle..." Jake let his voice trail off, remembering. Bob Duncan had been something else; he'd believed in "his" boys. Even when nobody else did.

Nick nodded. "I hear you."

The first time Jake had taken off for the hills, he'd been running away—back to Cheyenne or anywhere other than the boys' ranch he'd been sent to by some bleeding-heart judge. He hadn't expected to find his home in the wilds of Wyoming or discover a natural affinity for spaces undefined by other men. After that, he'd always been running *toward* something instead of away from it. Bob Duncan had seemed to understand that and had made sure Jake knew how to survive. He'd taught him the ways of the backwoods and hills.

"So my persuasive cousin managed to con you into this circus, as well," Nick said, drawing Jake back to the present.

"Yeah, well, it's for a good cause."

"So she informed me." Nick frowned and sipped at his coffee. "As she was dragging me out of bed and holding a gun to my head."

Jake smiled to himself, picturing young Lindsay Duncan manhandling her male cousin. Of course, Jake hadn't seen Lindsay in twelve years, so he imagined she didn't quite look the same as she had when he'd left Lost Springs. She'd been a spitfire then, and as much of a handful as any of Bob and Karen's other charges. "I was sorry to hear about your aunt and uncle," he said.

Nick nodded, tight-lipped. "They were good people."

"Yes, they were. But it looks like Lindsay and Rex are doing a good job of running the place for them."

"They're determined to keep it open." Nick shook his head. "Despite being dead broke."

"Can you blame them?"

"No. Not really."

"I must admit," Jake said, "when Lindsay called and told me about this auction, I thought she was nuts." He hadn't really wanted to come back to this place. Bob Duncan may have turned Jake's life around, but there were other memories here, bittersweet memories that Jake would have preferred to let lie. "But," he said, glancing around at the full tables, "she's drawn quite a crowd."

Nick followed Jake's gaze around the open pavilion and frowned. "My cousin isn't an easy woman to say no to."

"Tell me about it." Jake smiled wryly, remembering how Lindsay had tracked him down through a newspaper article and then relentlessly badgered him until he'd agreed to be one of her bonus bachelors.

"So, what are you doing now?" Nick asked, changing the subject abruptly. "Did you stay in the area after leaving the ranch?"

Jake hesitated, then realized that Nick had no idea how or when Jake had left the ranch. To the very end, Bob Duncan had been loyal to his boys, never betraying a trust. "No, I'm in Colorado. Outside Boulder."

"Still in the mountains?"

"We all have our places." But Jake didn't want to talk about his work, not even to Bob Duncan's nephew. Nodding toward the other man's uniform, he said, "I see you're still a marine. Special Ops?"

Nick shook his head. "Not anymore. I work for the Justice Department now. DEA. The uniform was

Lindsay's idea." With a snort of disgust he added, "She thought it might help her get a higher price for me."

Jake grinned, thinking that Lindsay had turned out to be just like her father. Determined and stubborn. "Well then," he said, lifting his coffee cup in salute. "Here's to the Duncans. All of them. And to letting the last of them put us on the auction block."

LOST SPRINGS RANCH WAS a short drive north of Lightning Creek, but before long Ali and Gail hit a steady stream of traffic. In this part of Wyoming, passing more than one other vehicle on the way to a neighboring ranch was an event, and that was usually a work-worn truck. Today, they followed two women in a blue Mercedes convertible with out-of-state plates, while behind them trailed a black Lincoln Town Car.

Fortunately, at the ranch itself, Lindsay had obviously planned for the crowd. Boys in bright orange vests directed the vehicles into long parking rows in one of the outside fields. Gail pulled in next to the Mercedes and shut off the engine. It was like being at Disney World, Ali thought, and she half expected a miniature trolley car to pick them up and cart them to the main event.

"Well," Gail said, nodding toward the striking woman who climbed from the expensive convertible. "I don't think you have to worry about the doctor or lawyer."

No, Ali thought, neither of them.

That didn't mean she wasn't worried. She still hadn't decided whether going through with this was a good idea or one of the most irresponsible things she'd ever done. Her carefully constructed plan, which had seemed so logical a few weeks ago, now felt totally unreasonable. And she couldn't for the life of her figure out what had ever made her think otherwise. Still, she knew she was going to go through with it, because if there was even a slight chance this would work, she had to try.

"Hey, Ali," Gail said, waving a hand in front of her face. "You still with me?"

Ali's cheeks heated. "Sorry."

"You okay?"

"Sure." Ali reached for the handle and opened the door. "I'm fine. Why wouldn't I be?" She climbed out of the truck, and after a moment's hesitation, Gail followed.

The ranch had a carnival atmosphere, with more expensive cars and trucks filling the field, and groups of people moving toward the ranch. There were kids everywhere, on the playground and racing among the groups of adults. Near the main house, a large tent had been set up with rows of picnic tables, and the smell of barbecue drifted on the air while Garth Brooks sang about being Mr. Right from overhead speakers.

Ali hadn't been to the ranch in more than twelve years, and then she'd never come by such a direct route or out in the open. Her excursions here had been made in secret. It seemed odd to be here now, and yet, it all felt too familiar. She wondered how the bachelors felt about coming back, the alumni who'd arrived here as troubled boys and left grown men? She thought about one boy in particular, a loner who'd spent more time in the woods than at the ranch itself. What would he remember? Who would he think of when he stepped back on these grounds?

Gail grabbed Ali's arm. "I want that."

Startled from her thoughts, Ali followed Gail's gaze to a table set up under the Converse County Hospital banner. Twyla McCabe stood talking to a man whom Ali recognized from the auction brochure. "What? The guy?"

"No, silly." Gail paused a moment, as if considering the idea. "Although, that is a thought. Tall. Dark. Sinfully handsome. What's not to like? You could do worse. But—" she shook her head "—it looks like Twyla's already got her sights set on him. Too bad."

Ali laughed, though it sounded forced even to her.

Gail didn't seem to notice. "Actually," she said, "I was talking about the quilt."

Behind Twyla, hanging from the branches of a massive oak, a lovely quilt swayed gently in the breeze. Ali didn't know much about quilts, but this one had an eye-catching design in a variety of soft colors.

"Come on," Gail said, and headed toward the table. They reached it just as the man walked away, leaving Twyla with a stack of tickets in her hand and looking a bit flushed.

"You okay, Twyla?" Gail asked, her eyes dancing with amusement.

Twyla pulled her gaze from the retreating male figure and turned to Gail. "He just bought a hundred dollars' worth of raffle tickets."

"Really?" Gail frowned at the man's back. "Darn. I guess there's no point in my buying any, then."

Twyla pulled herself together quickly. "Gail Sebring, what a thing to say. You know all the proceeds go to the hospital. And besides, you have every bit as much chance to win as anyone else.''

Gail laughed and held up her hands in defense. ''Okay, okay. I assume your mom and the ladies from the Quilt Quorum made it?''

Twyla smiled proudly. ''They do nice work, don't they.''

''I've been wanting one of their quilts forever. And it *is* a beauty.'' Gail sighed, and Ali knew her friend was hooked. ''Okay, I'll take five tickets.''

A few minutes later, after both of them had bought raffle tickets, Gail and Ali moved off toward the arena, where risers and a platform had been set up for the auction. If Ali had ever had any doubts about Gail knowing everybody in the county, she lost them then. They stopped to talk to at least a dozen people between Twyla's booth and the arena. Normally Ali wouldn't have minded; she would have welcomed the chance to get to know more people in the area. But today she couldn't keep her mind on casual conversation or remember half the people Gail introduced her to. Instead, she found herself watching the crowd, half of her hoping to spot a particular face while another part prayed she wouldn't.

Finally they made it to the auction area, and a teenage boy handed them a copy of the original brochure along with a thin, full-color flyer. When she glanced at it, Ali's heart skipped a beat.

''Hey, look at this,'' Gail said in reference to the flyer. ''Bonus bachelors.''

Ali knew all about the four bonus bachelors. They were last-minute additions to the lineup of successful Lost Springs alumni, and they were the reason her stomach had been coiled in knots for days. "Come on," she said, ignoring Gail's comment. "Let's find a seat."

The risers were filling up fast, and as Ali and Gail worked their way toward a couple of empty places, Ali wished she'd worn shorts or slacks. Climbing over people in a dress wasn't the easiest task in the world, and one more indication that she'd totally lost her mind by even coming to this auction.

As soon as they took their seats, Gail once again started pointing out people to Ali. "Look, there's Sugar Spinelli and Theda Duckworth in the front row," she said. "You remember them, don't you?"

Ali nodded absently. Who in Lightning Creek didn't know the wealthy and generous Sugar Spinelli. Or her best friend Theda Duckworth, who had once taught third grade at Lander Elementary.

"I wonder what they're up to?" Gail said with a mock frown. Then she nodded to her left and lowered her voice to a hushed whisper. "Oh, and look who else is here. Amelia Bainbridge-Campbell."

That was a new one on Ali. "Who is she?"

"Lightning Creek's Queen Bee herself. Or so she'd like to think," Gail added, "though she doesn't even live here. She's from somewhere out on the West Coast, Washington or Oregon, or somewhere like that."

Ali studied the austere older woman who held herself apart, sitting rigidly straight on the risers. "So what is she doing here?"

"Her husband was Bart Campbell," Gail explained. "He owned a very successful ranch a few miles out of town. When he died, he left the ranch to Amelia. Now she occasionally graces us with her presence and doles out charitable contributions to the needy.'' Gail rolled her eyes, apparently unimpressed by Amelia's generosity. ''I guess Lost Springs is on her list.''

Ali smiled at her friend's gossipy tone. Leave it to Gail to know not only everyone in town but all their secrets, as well. ''So who are the women with her?'' she asked. One was middle-aged and slightly overweight, but the other was young and pretty with French-braided blond hair, sunglasses and an amused expression that seemed out of place next to Amelia.

''I'm not sure,'' Gail said thoughtfully. ''But I think the older woman is her daughter Kathryn. I don't know the younger one. She certainly doesn't look like she belongs with Amelia, does she?''

''No,'' Ali said, thinking the blonde looked about as uncomfortable as Ali herself felt.

''Now, I really want to look at this,'' Gail said, as if she wasn't the one who'd been checking out the crowd. Starting to flip through the brochure, she added, ''You know, I haven't had time before now. Somehow I just couldn't bring myself to window-shop in front of John.''

Ali forced a smile, but Gail didn't seem to notice. ''So, have you picked one out?'' she asked. ''Oh, look at this. Wasn't he the guy we saw at Twyla's booth?''

Ali glanced down at a good-looking man in a tux, carrying a red rose. ''I think so.''

''What a hunk. And he's a doctor.'' She shook her head and flipped the page. ''Too bad Twyla has already staked her claim.'' Gail continued thumbing through the brochure, commenting on one bachelor after the other.

Ali's attention drifted to the crowd and the men milling around the platform. She didn't think she'd ever seen so many attractive men in one place in her life. Not that all of them were model perfect. There was just something about them, an air of confidence and assurance that made them a compelling group. She supposed Lindsay's parents could be given the credit for that. They'd evidently managed to take boys on the edge of trouble and turn them into upstanding adults. Not just one or two, but if the bios in the brochures could be believed, the Duncans had succeeded with at least sixteen of their once-wayward boys. That alone made this auction a worthy cause.

Then she saw him.

It happened just as Lindsay and the auctioneer got up on stage, but Ali hardly noticed. All she saw was a head of thick dark hair, broad shoulders and the flash of white when he smiled at the man next to him. She tried to look away, to listen as the auctioneer explained the rules, but the sight of him after so many years held her captive.

Until Gail grabbed her arm.

"You lied to me," she whispered as she shoved the flyer into Ali's hand. "This isn't about donating to a good cause. This is about Jake Merrill."

# CHAPTER TWO

As Jake took a seat, he suddenly realized what he'd let himself in for.

Until that moment, he hadn't really thought much about the auction itself, about climbing up on a stage in front of a bunch of strangers and having an auctioneer sell him to the highest bidder. All he'd been thinking about was repaying his debt to the Duncans by helping Lindsay keep the ranch.

Now he wondered if anyone would notice if he just disappeared.

Nearly two dozen men lingered near the platform, waiting for the auction to begin, while the risers filled with a crowd of mostly women. If Jake just got up and walked off, he'd be in his Jeep in less than two minutes and on his way back to Colorado. When the auctioneer got around to calling his name and no one responded, he'd make a joke about Jake getting cold feet and move on to the next victim. Jake would then send Lindsay a check to cover the lost donation.

Unfortunately, that wasn't how it was going to play out.

He'd given Lindsay his word, and he'd keep it no matter how uncomfortable this whole thing suddenly made him. Besides, the last time he'd run from Lost Springs, he vowed he'd never run from anything again. For twelve years he'd kept that promise, and he wasn't about to break it now.

Then Lindsay and the auctioneer climbed onstage, ending Jake's thoughts of escape.

The first bachelor in the lineup was Rob Carter.

Jake barely remembered the other man from their days at the ranch. A couple years ahead of Jake in school, Rob had been quieter and more studious than most of the other boys, though you couldn't tell that from the way he was handling himself onstage, smiling and playing to the crowd. The ladies were eating it up, and the bidding was getting intense.

Jake couldn't believe the figures being thrown out, and when the dollar amount topped the five-figure mark, he had to give Lindsay credit. She'd known what she was doing hosting a bachelor auction to raise cash for the ranch. And he was doubly glad he hadn't opted to head on back to Colorado. No way could he afford to match the money these women were willing to pay for a date.

When the bidding for Rob concluded, the winner was a silver-haired woman in a pink jogging suit. She and another member of the geriatric set jumped up and hugged each other, while Rob looked absolutely stunned. Jake smiled. Well, he thought, better an older woman who wanted a little dinner and dancing than someone young and hungry, looking for a lifetime commitment.

After that, another couple of bachelors, including Rex Trowbridge, were sold to the highest bidder. Lindsay won the bid for Rex, and Jake wondered about that. Neither of them seemed particularly dismayed by the prospect of a date.

Then it was Nick Petrocelli's turn, and Jake nodded

at the other man as he headed toward the stage. If the bidding so far was any indication, Lindsay would be right about those marine dress blues. They were likely to bring a hefty sum. And Nick looked the part. He might be working for the Justice Department, but he was all soldier today, standing with his feet planted firmly apart and his arms folded behind his back.

As Jake predicted, the bidding went a little wild, then ended with a hush as a stately older woman stood up and offered a year's tuition at the University of Wyoming for one of the ranch boys. Of course, no one topped the offer, and Nick went off to meet his "date."

After that, with each bachelor who climbed onstage, the crowd got a little wilder and more raucous. As one of the four bachelors added to the lineup at the last minute, Jake knew he'd be among the last called. He hated to think how wound-up the crowd would be by the time they got to him. Or maybe, if he was lucky, they'd run out of money by then.

Before Jake was anywhere near ready, the auctioneer said, "And our next bachelor is…" He paused dramatically, as if waiting for a drumroll. "Jake Merrill."

"What the hell," Jake muttered, and stood.

"Go get 'em," someone behind him yelled.

Jake groaned, forced a smile and made his way up to the podium. Following Carter's lead, he leaned over and kissed Lindsay on the cheek. "This is your idea of revenge, isn't it?" he whispered. "For all of us who tormented you as kids."

Lindsay grinned and patted him on the cheek. "You bet."

The audience, primed and ready, hooted and howled.

"Okay, ladies," urged the auctioneer. "Let's hear it for Jake."

The crowd applauded, and Jake turned, laughing— at Lindsay and the whole absurdity of the situation. Women. He'd never much understood them, but he sure did love 'em. And this whole crazy auction reminded him how much.

"Let me tell you about Jake," the auctioneer called over the noise. "He's twenty-nine and a Scorpio, so you don't want to cross him."

The audience laughed.

"And get this, Jake works for the Forest Service as a Mountain Rescue Squad coordinator." Turning to Jake, he added, "I'm impressed. Tell us, isn't that dangerous?" He held out the microphone.

Jake stepped forward. "Sometimes. But mostly—"

Before he could finish, the microphone disappeared and the auctioneer was again talking to the women in the audience. "Dangerous, indeed. What do you think, ladies? Does Jake look like he can handle 'dangerous'?"

"You bet," someone called out, and everyone laughed and broke into rowdy applause.

Jake laughed right along with them, again wondering how the hell he'd gotten himself into this. Knowing the answer, he threw Lindsay a glance, and she smiled back with an expression that said, "You ain't seen nothing yet."

Sure enough, the auctioneer wasn't done with him. "Jake, it says here that your biggest achievement was rescuing two wolf cubs from a pack of wild dogs."

The other man focused on the audience as they let out a loud collective sigh.

Jake shook his head. When he'd told Lindsay to fill out his auction sheet any way she wanted, he hadn't realized she'd be so creative.

When the crowd calmed down, the auctioneer went on. "Jake drives a four-wheel-drive Jeep, and his favorite song is 'Rescue Me.'

"His most embarrassing moment was when he emerged from a mountain stream in the altogether..." The auctioneer coughed and hesitated, feigning his own embarrassment. "Only to find a Girl Scout troop camped on the shore."

Pandemonium broke out: laughter, applause, wolf whistles. Someone yelled, "Let's hear it for the Girl Scouts."

Imagination, my foot, Jake thought. Lindsay was downright sadistic.

Over the noise, the auctioneer continued, "His ideal woman is someone who can keep up with him. And the five words Jake uses to describe himself are..." He waited for the crowd to calm down. "You ladies ready for this?" Arching his eyebrows, he surveyed the crowd and said each word with deliberate slowness. "Rugged. Wild. Ready. And. Willing."

Again the crowd went a little crazy, and the auctioneer had to yell to be heard over them. "What about it, ladies? Who wants Jake Merrill to rescue her?"

All in fun and for a good cause, Jake told himself as he threw another glance at Lindsay, who gave him a thumbs-up as she laughed and applauded with the crowd.

The bidding started and Jake lost track of who bid

what. There was a middle-aged woman in a short denim skirt and fringed vest, the blonde in the tight white jeans, and a woman sitting mostly hidden behind one of the few men in the crowd. The only thing he could see of her was the bottom half of a pair of long, slender legs. Finally, it was down to the woman with the great legs and the one with the fringed vest. Every time one bid, the other upped it until he began to wonder where these women got this kind of money. For a date.

Finally, fringed vest shook her head and spoke loud enough for everyone to hear. "Darn, if this ain't too rich for my blood. He's all yours, honey."

The crowd laughed, and the auctioneer called, "Do I hear five hundred more?" When no one responded, he brought the gavel down with a bang. "Sold to the pretty lady in peach."

Jake bowed slightly, threw Lindsay one final you-owe-me-for-this look and hopped off the stage, glad it was finally over. As he passed the next guy whose name was called, Jake shot the other man a sympathetic smile. "It's all yours, buddy."

He headed over to the cashier's table, where he figured he'd meet his new "owner" and find out the details of their date. He was laughing and joking with the girl taking the money, when she looked at someone behind him and smiled.

"Hey, Dr. Kendrick," she said. "You come to pay *me* for a change?"

Jake turned toward the soft feminine laugh behind him and felt the ground shift beneath his feet. His body recognized her before his mind accepted her presence. Tall and slender, with hair the color of wild mink and eyes the coppery fineness of autumn leaves, she was the girl who'd haunted his dreams for the past twelve years. Only this woman was no longer a girl. And neither belonged here: not the girl in this time, nor the woman in this place.

"Hello, Jake," she said in that soft Southern voice of hers that had always seemed so exotic and out of place in Wyoming.

"Ali?" He knew he sounded like an idiot, felt like one, too, but he didn't have any words. Hell, he hardly had a voice. *What was she doing here?*

"How have you been?" she asked.

He found his voice, though it sounded strange, disoriented. "Fine. You?"

"I've been good." Turning to the cashier, she said, "I suppose you'll take a check."

"Sure."

"Check?" Jake said at the same time.

"I don't usually carry that kind of cash with me," Ali answered, winking at the cashier. Then she leaned over to use the tabletop to write her check. She wore a simple dress, slender and peach-colored.

"Wait a minute," he said.

She looked up at him expectantly. "What is it?"

"You're the..." *Woman who won the bid.*

"I'm the one who bought you. Yes. And you didn't even recognize me." She straightened, shook her head and tsked. "I'm crushed." She didn't look anything near crushed, Jake thought. In fact, she looked as if she was laughing at him. "But then again, it *has* been a long time. Hasn't it?"

"Ali..." He still couldn't make sense of her being here.

But she was on a roll, and there was a coldness in

her eyes that hadn't been there years earlier. "I think it was twelve years ago, to be exact."

"Twelve years?"

"As I remember—" her voice was as hard and cold as her eyes "—you left me at the altar." She smiled, though that, too, held an undeniable chill. "So to speak."

AN HOUR LATER, after a long, silent drive home, Gail stood in the middle of Ali's kitchen, her eyes sparking with anger. "So, when were you going to tell me?"

Ali didn't have a good answer, one that would erase the hurt on her friend's face. All she could offer was the truth. "I was afraid you'd try and talk me out of it."

"You're darn right I would have talked you out of it."

"I know you never liked Jake—"

"That's not true. I always liked Jake. Every girl in town liked Jake. I just never trusted him." Then, crossing her arms, she added, "But this has nothing to do with my opinion of Jake Merrill. It's about you and what he did to you."

Ali sighed and moved over to the kitchen table, where she collapsed in a chair. It had been a long, nerve-racking day, and she wasn't sure her legs would hold her much longer. "That was twelve years ago, Gail."

"He left you alone and pregnant."

"He didn't know about Sam."

"And that's supposed to excuse him?" Gail followed Ali over to the table and sat in the chair across from her. "Ali, you were ready to give up everything for him. Your family, your schooling, your entire future. And he—''

''I know,'' Ali said, cutting her off. She'd been young and foolish, falling in love with him, giving him her virginity, planning to run away with him, and then waiting in a rainstorm for two hours past the time he'd promised to meet her.

''Heaven only knows how much longer you would have waited for him if I hadn't come after you,'' Gail said, as if reading her mind. Then, never one to mince words, she added, ''He used you, Ali, and then left you.''

Ali flinched, though it was the truth—a truth she'd come to terms with a long time ago. But there was another truth she'd come to accept, as well. ''Did it ever occur to you that he did me a favor by not showing up?''

''No,'' Gail answered. ''And I doubt it occurred to him, either.''

''Think about it,'' Ali insisted. As the one other person who knew about Ali's relationship with Jake, Gail tended to see only the pain he'd caused her friend. ''Where would Sam and I be if I'd run off and married Jake Merrill?''

After a moment's hesitation, Gail nodded reluctantly. ''Okay, so looking back, it was probably a good thing he never showed up. You and Sam are better off without him. Still, that doesn't excuse what he did. Or explain why you're intent on this crazy scheme of yours.''

''I know you're angry that I didn't tell you, but this is something I have to do.''

''Why?''

Ali hesitated, knowing Gail—who'd married her

high school sweetheart and had two rambunctious but wonderful boys, and whose life was so normal she could star in a Hallmark commercial—wasn't going to understand. "I need to put him behind me."

Gail started to speak but Ali held up a hand and said, "Let me finish. For twelve years I've been living with the memory of Jake Merrill, and it's kept me from getting on with my life." She hesitated a moment, gathering her thoughts, and then went on. "I know that doesn't make much sense, considering he lied and ran out on me, but it's a fact." She paused again before saying, "There's never been anyone else."

"No one?"

Ali shook her head.

"Well, you've been busy," Gail said. "Between school and raising Samantha, you haven't had much time for—"

Ali cut her off. "That's what I used to tell myself, as well. But the fact is, I've had opportunities, plenty of them. I just haven't been interested. After a date or two, I always end up comparing the man of the moment to Jake. Is he as handsome? As exciting? As smart?" She shrugged, knowing how crazy she sounded. "None of them ever measure up."

Gail shook her head. "You don't give them a chance."

"Exactly." Ali leaned forward on the table. "My memories of Jake are distorted. I was seventeen and in love for the first time. He's the father of my child. And every man I've met since has had to compete. Not with reality, but with a memory. It's not rational but it's the way it is." She sat back in her chair, taking a moment to gather her resolve. "This is my chance, Gail, to change that."

"By going off alone with him for a weekend?"

"I'm going to get to know the real Jake Merrill. The man who used me, lied to me and walked out on me. And I'm going to prove to myself that he can't possibly measure up to my memories of him."

For the first time in days, Ali was sure of herself, sure of her decision. Maybe she should have talked to Gail sooner. There was something about putting an idea into words that made everything clearer. Or maybe it had just been seeing Jake again and having her old anger surface. Whatever the cause, it felt good to be herself again, to be confident about what she was doing.

"Are you sure this isn't about revenge?" Gail asked.

"Revenge?"

"You know, to show him how well you turned out, how successful you are without him."

"That's ridiculous."

Gail tilted her head and narrowed her eyes. "Is it?"

"Yes." A small voice inside Ali asked if she was being totally honest. Could part of this be about revenge? About showing him the woman she'd become? No, she didn't believe that. "I'm doing this to put him behind me, Gail. And that's the *only* reason I'm doing it."

For a moment, neither of them spoke. Then Gail said, "What if you can't? What if your plan backfires?"

"Backfires?" It took Ali a moment to realize what Gail meant. What if after all these years and the way he'd betrayed her, Ali still wanted Jake Merrill? Just the thought made her confidence slip a notch. She remembered her first glimpse of him at the auction, his smile, and the way he'd handled himself onstage, laughing along with the crowd. She recalled wondering when he'd gotten so tall and his shoulders so broad. He'd been the best-looking boy in town all those years ago, and she'd fallen fast and hard. But that had been no boy on the stage today. He was a grown man with all the promise of that long-ago boy fulfilled.

What if she once again fell under his spell?

A corner of her mind whispered a warning, but she pushed it aside.

Jake might no longer be a boy, but she was no longer an innocent girl, either. He'd made sure of that the day he'd run off without her. And despite her brave words about how much better off she and Sam were without him, a part of her still mourned his desertion—a part of her she'd learned to shield and protect with anger.

She drew on that anger now.

"That's not going to happen," she said, answering Gail's question with as much confidence as she could muster.

"Are you sure?"

Before she could respond, the back door slammed open and three miniature whirlwinds and one oversize hound blew into the kitchen.

"Mom, we're back," Sam said, as if there was any doubt. "Hey, Aunt Gail."

The boys echoed Sam's greeting and all four headed toward the refrigerator.

"What's to eat?" Paul asked as Sam yanked open the door.

"I'm starved," Roy, his younger brother, added.

"Whoa," Gail said, grabbing her eldest by the shoulder. "Where's your dad?"

"He went home." Paul squirmed out of his mother's grasp and joined Sam as she retrieved bread and sandwich meat from the refrigerator.

"Home?" Gail glanced at the back door in disbelief. "He just dropped you off and went home?"

"Yeah." Sam threw Gail a quick grin. "He said he had to get back to work."

"I think we wore him out," Roy chimed in.

Ali laughed, though her insides ached with envy over the normalcy of Gail's life. She'd go home and give John hell for dropping the kids off when he'd promised to watch them all day. But in the end, they'd kiss and make up, because Gail knew John would always be there for her and their boys.

Ali wanted the same for herself and her daughter. A husband. A father. Someone they could love and trust. Someone who wouldn't run out on them. That's why she had to face Jake Merrill, had to replace her memories with reality, because only then could she move on with her life.

"I guess you got your wish," she said, smiling and dismissing her momentary bout of envy. Gail deserved the best no matter how Ali's situation turned out. "He now knows what you go through every day."

"Why, that—"

Ali cleared her throat and nodded toward the kids.

Gail pressed her lips together and shook her head. "Just wait until I get home."

Ali laughed again and went to help Sam with the sandwiches, more to keep her from totally demolishing the kitchen than because the eleven-year-old couldn't manage on her own. A few minutes later the three kids and the dog exited the back door as quickly and loudly as they'd entered, leaving both mothers a bit off balance in their wake.

"She looks just like him," Gail said in the sudden silence.

Surprised, Ali turned toward her friend, ready to deny it. Then she sighed. What was the point in denying the obvious? "Yes, she does. I didn't realize how much until…" Until she'd seen Jake today.

"Those eyes and that hair." Gail shook her head and sighed. "Are you going to tell her about him?"

Ali stiffened and moved to start cleaning up the kids' mess. "I don't know."

"She deserves to know her father, Ali."

"We've managed just fine for the past twelve years without him." Her voice sounded petty and strained, but she couldn't seem to help herself. Gail had hit on something Ali had been avoiding thinking about for weeks. All her life she'd prided herself on facing things head-on. Even at seventeen, pregnant and husbandless, she'd dealt with the situation without denying her responsibility. Yet in the last few weeks, as she'd planned her reunion with Jake Merrill, she hadn't allowed herself to consider the consequences to Sam of finding her father.

"I don't see where anything has changed," she said.

"You're kidding, right?" There was no humor in Gail's voice. "Everything's changed."

Ali stopped and looked at her friend as a rush of guilt washed over her.

From the very beginning she'd told Sam the truth

about her father. Sam knew her parents had broken up before Ali found out about her pregnancy, and that Jake had moved out of the area. Later, Ali hadn't known where to reach him to tell him he had a daughter. Jake didn't know about Sam, so she couldn't feel unwanted or unloved by her father.

It had been so easy.

That had all changed the day Lindsay Duncan had asked Ali to participate in the auction, and Ali had seen Jake's name on the list of bachelors. She should have thought of Sam right then.

"And what about Jake?" Gail said. "Lord knows, I still get angry when I think about how he left you. But he deserves to know he has a daughter."

"I doubt he cares."

"You don't know that, Ali."

For a few minutes, she didn't respond. Gail was right. Again. Ali had no idea how Jake would react to finding out he had a daughter. She'd thought she knew him twelve years ago and had been dead wrong. How could she possibly predict how he would react now? He might be the father of her child, but he was a stranger.

With a sigh, she nodded. "Okay, Gail, I'll think about it."

Gail started to say something else but obviously thought better of it. They worked together in tense silence for a few minutes more, putting the kitchen back in order. Then Gail asked, "What are you going to tell Sam when you go up to the cabin with Jake?"

Without looking at her friend, Ali said, "It's the weekend of the camp-out." Every year the seventh and eighth graders from Lander Elementary went on a weekend camping trip in the mountains.

Gail nodded. "Oh, that's right. I forgot." Again silence fell between them, and Ali braced herself for more questions. But Gail surprised her by simply retrieving her purse and saying, "Well, I'm going to collect my two heathens and head home." She started for the door, stopped and said, "I sure hope you know what you're doing, Ali."

Ali looked at her friend as a feeling of dread settled over her. "Me, too."

# CHAPTER THREE

THREE WEEKS OF MISERY.

That's how Jake thought of the time that had passed since Ali had bought him at the Lost Springs bachelor auction. But this morning, when he'd climbed into his Jeep and headed back to Wyoming to keep his end of the bargain, he knew his torment had just begun. A weekend alone in the mountains— that's what she wanted, what she'd bought and paid for.

The only question was why.

He'd turned it over in his head a million times since that day at the ranch and still hadn't come up with an answer that made sense. The only thing he knew for certain was that Ali's presence at the auction had been no accident. She'd known he would be there and had planned to bid on him. He'd seen that in her eyes and in the silent disapproval of her friend Gail, who'd stood like a sentry, glaring at him while he and Ali had exchanged the few words necessary to arrange their date.

Now, still without any answers, he was on his way north to a cabin somewhere in the Laramie Mountains, to spend forty-eight hours with a woman who had every reason in the world to hate him. If Ali was out to punish him, she couldn't have picked a better method.

It hadn't always been that way. There had been a time when he'd wanted to spend every waking moment with her. Then, for years after he'd left Lost Springs, he'd imagine seeing her again. He'd daydream about running into her unexpectedly and explaining things to her, and she'd understand and forgive him. But it had been a long while since he'd indulged in such fantasies, and over the years he'd come to accept that he'd done the right thing by leaving, even if he hadn't done it in the most honorable way. At the time, he'd been capable of nothing else. Now he figured the best thing for both of them was to let the past alone.

Unfortunately, she didn't seem to agree.

So what did she want from him? A date? A weekend to reminisce about old times? He didn't think so. But he had no choice but to honor his promise and face her. The way he should have done twelve years ago. So he kept his Jeep pointed north and vowed he'd get through this weekend. Whatever it entailed.

A half hour past Cheyenne it started to rain, slowing him down and adding to his already dismal mood. It was late afternoon by the time he reached his destination. Pulling into the clearing surrounding the mountain cabin, he stopped and sat for a moment with the engine running and the wipers swishing against the windshield. Even after he'd shut off the ignition, he made no move to get out. Instead, he remained in the relative safety of the vehicle while checking out the surroundings.

The cabin sat on a gradual slope of the mountain with its back to a forest of ponderosa, limber and lodgepole pines. Large and sprawling, the building was of modern log construction with a wide front porch and natural stone chimney. The clearing wrapped around three sides of the structure, opening the forest to the sun.

Today, however, there was only rain.

While he sat there, the front door opened and Ali stepped out onto the porch. Across the rain-drenched space, his gaze locked with hers and everything else fell away: the distance, the years, the pain they'd caused each other. Unlike the day at the ranch, she wore jeans and a soft-looking sweater the color of early morning sunshine. It lightened the gray afternoon and made her look younger, more like the girl he'd once known than the sophisticated woman he'd met at the auction. In that instant, she was his Ali again, the girl he'd known and loved a lifetime ago. Then just as quickly, the impression vanished. She took a step back, and he felt her withdrawal like a slap.

He deserved that, he supposed. But why this? Why bring him here to this out-of-the-way place for a weekend? If she were any other woman, he might think this was some form of revenge. But not Ali. He couldn't believe she'd changed that much over the past twelve years. Besides, she had no idea how difficult this was for him, how much just bringing him here would make him suffer. As far as she knew, he'd left her because he didn't care. Not because he cared too much.

"Damn," he mumbled, and reached into the back seat to grab his overnight bag. He might as well get moving; he wouldn't get any answers sitting here. Turning up his collar, he darted out into the rain. Ali took another step back as he scrambled up onto the porch, stamping his feet and shaking the water from his shoulders.

"Sorry I'm late," he said as he opened his jacket and shoved his rain-drenched hair off his face. "The weather slowed me down and I missed one of the turns."

"I wasn't sure you'd show."

Her words stopped him cold. After a long, tense moment, he said, "I told you I'd be here."

"As I remember, that doesn't always mean anything."

At that, Jake seriously considered picking up his bag and heading on back to Colorado. He didn't need to listen to a woman taking potshots at him all weekend long. The only problem was, she was right. He'd promised to meet her once before and hadn't shown up. How could he defend himself against that kind of truth?

Before he could even try, she said, "I'm sorry. That was uncalled-for."

"No, that's okay. I deserved it." *And more.* Though he hadn't expected her to dish it out with such ease. Maybe this was about revenge, after all, or at least about making him feel damn uncomfortable. If so, she was succeeding.

"Come inside," she said. "I built a fire." She turned toward the door, but he snagged her arm to stop her.

"Ali?"

She glanced down at his hand, and he immediately released her, though the feel of her slender arm remained etched on his palm. Then she lifted her gaze back to his, and for a moment, he thought he saw a trace of the girl she'd been all those years ago. With her unusual cinnamon-colored eyes and skin like fresh cream, she seemed little older than the seventeen she'd been then. But he only had to look deeper, to the coolness and anger shimmering just below the surface, to know she wasn't the Ali he'd known.

This lovely woman was a stranger.

He backed up and asked, "What am I doing here?"

"I bought you at a bachelor auction." Her sarcasm was new, too; another side to this woman he didn't know. "Remember?"

"That's not what I'm talking about," he snapped, though he hadn't meant to. The weeks of wondering were beginning to wear on him. Purposely softening his tone, he added, "Why did you—" he made a sweeping gesture with his hand "—arrange this?"

She hesitated, and her expression thawed somewhat. "Come inside, Jake. It's wet and cold out here, and I have a fire going inside."

"I want—"

She held up a hand to interrupt him. "I know. We'll talk later." Her voice wrapped around him, its slow Southern tones like warm honey. "I promise."

He considered that for a moment, then nodded. He'd waited three weeks; he could wait a few more hours. Besides, what choice did he have? He'd given his word to Lindsay when he'd agreed to be one of her bonus bachelors, and to Ali when she'd bought and paid for him.

Whatever game she was playing, he'd go along. After all, he just needed to make it through the weekend. Two days and nights. Less than forty-eight hours. Then he could return to his life in Colorado and once again relegate Ali Kendrick to his past.

He followed her inside the cabin, which was as

impressive as the outside and equally suited to the Wyoming mountains. Wide open with polished hardwood floors, tongue-and-groove paneling and a beamed ceiling, the cabin's great room conveyed a sense of bringing the forest indoors. The large stone fireplace took up the entire south wall with a furniture grouping in soft natural colors positioned in front. Straight ahead was an airy kitchen, eating nook and hallway that disappeared into the back. On the right, a polished oak staircase ascended to an open balcony that ran the entire length of the first floor.

Leave it to Ali and her family to own or rent a getaway cabin that cost more than most people's homes. "Nice place," he said. "Is it yours?"

"It is now."

At his questioning look, she added, "It was my grandfather's." She put distance between them by moving across the room to the kitchen.

"Was?"

"He died about five years ago."

"I'm sorry." He'd liked her grandfather, though it hadn't been mutual. The old man had never trusted Jake, and with good reason. "I know how close you two were."

"Thanks." She acknowledged his sympathy with a nod and a tight smile. "But he had a good life, did just as he pleased up until the very end." Her smile softened, became almost wistful. "He built this cabin a few years before he died. He said Lightning Creek was getting too crowded." She laughed quietly. "Can you imagine?"

Jake grinned, remembering Austin Kendrick, a tall lanky cowboy who'd made good on the rodeo circuit then retired to Lightning Creek to raise his son,

Charles—Ali's father. Austin had always been a loner, living by his own rules with little tolerance for outsiders. Few people would understand how he could think a town with a population of two thousand was becoming too crowded. But Jake did.

"Actually," she said, bringing Jake out of his thoughts, "it was *his* money that paid for our date."

"Really?" Jake dropped his bag next to the door and crossed his arms. "Do you think he would have approved?"

Ignoring his question she said, "In his will, he specified a certain amount of money be donated to charitable organizations benefitting Wyoming. As executor of his estate, I figured Lost Springs Ranch qualified."

"Somehow I don't think he would have liked the side benefits." Jake moved away from the door into the warm expanse of wood that made up the room. Now that he knew the cabin had belonged to her grandfather, he could see the old man's mark on the place. He'd had a gift with wood, for taking a rough piece and turning it into something beautiful. There were several carvings scattered around the room: a bear, a mountain cat and a magnificent bull elk that Jake suspected would bring in more than his monthly paycheck if Ali ever attempted to sell it. "I wasn't exactly his first choice for his granddaughter."

She shrugged, went to the stove and lifted the lid off a large pot, releasing the fragrant aroma of cooking spices. "You might be surprised." Then, nodding toward the hallway, she added, "You can put your stuff away in the back. There are two downstairs bedrooms. Take your pick."

"Where are you sleeping?" He asked the question before he could stop himself.

Her gaze snapped to his, and a spark of memory arced between them, sending a surge of warmth straight to his groin. Then her eyes turned as frosty as a January morning. "There's a third bedroom upstairs."

It took him a moment, but he forced a shrug, pretending indifference and dismissing the question and her response as if he hadn't just put his foot in his mouth. "Just wanted to make sure I didn't claim the wrong room."

She arched an eyebrow, letting him know she understood exactly what he'd meant and what she thought of the idea.

Before he could dig himself a deeper hole, Jake retrieved his overnight bag and made his way down the hallway toward the back bedrooms. Both were large and comfortable, like the rest of the cabin, and furnished with two double beds. He dumped his small suitcase on one of the beds and silently cursed himself.

*How stupid could he be?*

What had he been thinking—asking her where she was sleeping as if he actually expected the two of them to share more than one long, uncomfortable weekend. For weeks he'd thought of little else but Ali, questioning why she'd resurfaced in his life and forced him into this weekend. Now he had to admit that part of his disquiet had been due to the memories that had haunted him day and night. He'd tried to push them aside, tried not to remember, not to think about how it would feel to hold her again, love her again. He'd thought he had succeeded, but evidently he'd been fooling himself. Despite everything that had passed between them, despite her anger and the fact he hardly knew the woman she'd become, he still wanted her.

Obviously, Ali had no such thoughts. *Whatever* she'd brought him here for, it had nothing to do with reviving their past affair.

He cursed himself again.

This whole charade was getting to him. But he'd promised to go through with this weekend and he'd keep his word. He'd run from Ali once before; he wasn't going to do it again. He would just have to be careful that he didn't do anything even more foolish.

Opening his bag, he dug out a dry shirt and made quick work of changing, not allowing himself to linger in the quiet room. Whatever else was going to happen between the two of them in the next two days, whatever needed saying, he wanted to get on with it so he could move on with his life.

AS JAKE LEFT THE ROOM, Ali put the lid back on the pot of chili and backed away from the stove. Closing her eyes, she took a couple of deep breaths, then looked down at her hands. They were trembling.

*Stupid. Stupid. Stupid.*

Whatever had made her think bringing Jake here was a good idea? She must have temporarily lost her mind. Lord knew she'd had enough signs to that effect, but now sanity had returned and she was stuck with it.

She'd been a wreck all day, getting up a full hour earlier than usual to feed and tend the animals in her care before transporting them to Doc Martin's clinic. Fortunately she had no sick patients at the moment, and her only boarders were a pair of poodles belonging to an older couple who'd gone back east for a family emergency.

Still, nothing had gone smoothly.

One of the small dogs got it into his head that Chester was a threat, and went a little crazy at the sight of the big shepherd. The poodle yapped and created a ruckus until he made himself ill. Ali had to first take time to close Chester in the house, then clean up after the small dog and calm him down before loading him into his carrier. By the time she returned from Doc Martin's to rouse Sam and get her ready for her camping trip, Ali was running a half hour late.

And then, of course, Sam had been in rare form.

Always full of energy and mischief, she was even more so today. Ali knew it was because of the upcoming outing, which her daughter had been looking forward to for weeks, but that didn't make dealing with her any easier. She argued with her mother about everything from eating breakfast to whether or not she could take Chester with her for the weekend. At one point, Ali decided she was definitely going nuts, but finally they were ready. She drove Sam over to meet Gail, who was one of the drivers and chaperons for the group of campers.

"Good luck," Ali said to Gail as the two overly excited preteens started loading their gear into the back of Gail's Bronco. "I don't envy you this tour of duty."

Gail grinned. "Don't be so smug. Next year's your turn, and they'll be closer to adolescence."

Ali laughed and started toward her car, eager to get going. Gail followed, and when they were out of earshot of the kids, she said, "What have you decided about Sam and Jake?"

A tinge of irritation struck Ali at the question. She was already feeling guilty enough about this; she didn't need Gail's reminder. Then she let it go. Gail meant well. "I decided you were right. They deserve to know each other."

"Good." Gail nodded approvingly. "When are you going to tell them?"

"Pushy, aren't you?"

Gail smiled and shrugged. "Just watching out for my best friend."

Ali couldn't argue with that. "I'm going to tell Jake first and gauge his reaction. I don't want to raise Sam's hopes about meeting her father only to find out he's not interested."

Gail thought about that for a moment "Then I think you're the one who's going to need luck this weekend, not me." With that she'd hugged Ali and sent her on her way.

Gail's statement came back to Ali now as she got herself under control and began to set the table. Gail had said she needed luck. In Ali's mind, luck wasn't what she needed. She needed to go back in time and forget this crazy scheme of hers. And if that weren't possible, a shrink might be helpful.

After leaving Gail, Ali had headed for the mountains. She'd arrived about ten and spent the rest of the day cleaning the cabin—even though it was already spotless. She never left the place without putting everything in order. Usually she simply pulled off the old sheets covering the furniture, brought in a fresh supply of wood for the fireplace and started something cooking to make the cabin warm and comfortable. Today, she'd done all that and more. She'd changed linens that had never been slept in, freshened bathrooms that were already clean, and polished furniture that already shone. She wanted to stay busy, to keep from dwelling on the approaching evening and her arriving guest. But all the cleaning in the world couldn't put Jake out of her thoughts.

She had supposed her case of the jitters was only natural. After all, she was about to spend a weekend alone with an attractive man, a man she'd once loved and who had fathered her child. The fact he'd walked out on her only made the situation more nerve-racking. But she figured she'd calm down soon enough. A few hours in Jake's company was all it would take. The man would dispel her illusions about the boy, and that would be the end of it. She'd forget Jake Merrill and get on with her life.

She'd realized her mistake the moment he arrived.

He'd clambered up onto her front porch—large, wet and overwhelmingly male—and she'd known she was in trouble. That's when she acknowledged that it was the man himself who was the problem, whose mere presence put her on edge and made her want things she shouldn't want. And that by bringing him here, she might have made forgetting him harder than ever.

Gail had been right. This whole thing had been a bad idea.

"Smells good."

Ali's heart lurched as she spun around to find Jake standing in the doorway. "Damn it, Jake."

He started toward her, concern etched on his face. "I'm sorry. I didn't mean to startle you."

She held up a hand to keep him from coming

closer. "No, it's okay." With a deep breath, she willed her heartbeat to return to normal. "I just didn't hear you coming."

He smiled apologetically and stuck his hands into the back pockets of his jeans. "Next time I'll whistle or something."

"That should do it." She nodded, feeling silly and suddenly very aware of the small kitchen with him standing in the middle of it, taking up so much space.

He'd changed into a dry shirt and combed his damp hair. He was impossibly handsome, the simple white shirt setting off his dark features and broad shoulders, the jeans, snug and well-worn, emphasizing his narrow hips and muscular thighs. He looked better than any man had a right to look—which didn't help to slow down her pulse.

A smile crept across his face, and she realized she was staring. A flush of heat singed her cheeks, and she quickly turned back to the stove.

"I hope you like chili," she said, trying to keep her voice detached, but it sounded a little breathless even to her.

"Love it."

She thought she detected a smile in his voice. *Was he laughing at her?*

"I thought it would taste good on a rainy night."

He moved up behind her. "What can I do to help?" He smelled as wonderful as he looked, damp and male, with a hint of some spicy masculine aftershave.

"Nothing." Her voice still sounded odd, and while he stood so close, she doubted whether she could correct it. All she could do was hope he didn't notice. "Everything's ready. Why don't you sit down?"

She stirred the chili one last time, replaced the lid and grabbed a couple of pot holders. Before she could lift the pot, however, he stepped up beside her.

"Here," he said, reaching past her. "Let me."

She thought about arguing with him, but decided putting distance between them was the easiest route. And the safest. She backed up, wondering why she had to notice things about him that she never noticed about other men—like the play of muscles beneath his shirt as he lifted the large pot and carried it to the table, or the way his dark hair lay against his collar, just a little too long.

Angry at herself for such adolescent foolishness, she turned back to the oven and pulled out the tray of fresh rolls she'd been keeping warm. Placing them in a napkin-lined basket, she steeled herself against her own wayward hormones. Then she joined Jake at the table, where he'd already dished out two full bowls of the chili. Sitting down, she forced herself not to look at the man across from her and began eating.

After a few minutes of awkward silence, Jake said, "This is really good."

"You sound surprised."

"No." He looked embarrassed. "It's just that it's been a while since I've had a home-cooked meal. I pretty much live on frozen dinners, with an occasional burger from the local bar."

"I take it you don't cook."

"Not hardly." He refilled his bowl and took another couple of rolls from the basket. "How about you? You used to hate anything that kept you indoors."

She shrugged. Having a child had a way of changing you, but she wasn't ready to tell him about Sam yet. There was information she wanted from him first. "I've learned a lot of things over the last twelve years." She said it without rancor, without thinking, but the reference to the past brought a wariness to his expression she couldn't miss. They were virtually strangers despite their past, and she'd all but dragged him to this out-of-the-way place without explanation. She saw the questions in his eyes and felt his discomfort charge the air.

Shaking her head apologetically, she said, "I didn't mean anything by that."

He nodded and looked away. "It's okay. We're bound to step on each other's toes a bit."

Again the silence fell around them, heavy and awkward.

After a few minutes, Jake said, "The cashier at the auction called you 'doctor,' which I'm guessing means you got through vet school."

"Yes." Evidently he was trying to find a neutral topic, and Ali appreciated the effort. "A couple of years ago."

"Congratulations. I always knew you could do it."

She looked at him, surprised by the sincerity in his voice, and smiled. "Thank you. It was tough, and there were times—" She stopped herself abruptly. She'd been about to tell him how hard school had been, especially while raising a daughter. A part of her wanted him to know how well she'd done without him, and her cheeks heated with the realization. Again, one of Gail's warnings had hit too close for comfort. She shouldn't care what Jake Merrill thought about her, but she did.

"Are you practicing in Lightning Creek?"

She nodded. "I'm working with Doc Martin. It would have been tough getting started otherwise."

"How so?"

"It's a small town and I'm an outsider. An unknown." She shrugged, thinking he of all people should see the obvious. After all, he'd been an outsider in Lightning Creek himself. "The ranchers in particular aren't inclined to trust me, especially being a woman."

"That can't be easy."

"It's working out okay. Doc Martin is getting up in years, and though he's not quite ready to retire, he's ready to slow down. So we made a deal."

He nodded, urging her to continue.

"I work in town at his office a couple of mornings a week and board the animals who need overnight care in a kennel next to my house. In exchange, Doc's turned over his out-of-office practice to me, and I make the rounds of the neighboring ranches."

"Sounds like he's gotten the better end of the bargain."

"Not really. With his endorsement, I've gained ground with the locals that would have taken me years to acquire on my own. If at all.

"What about you?" she asked, directing the conversation away from herself. "Is any of what that auctioneer said true?"

He smiled, a sexy, crooked smile. "Only the part about my working on a mountain rescue team."

"Isn't that dangerous?" She couldn't help but tease him a bit.

He frowned, then must have realized she was joking, because he laughed and said, "Yeah, about as dangerous as gelding a stallion. If you don't know what you're doing…"

"…you'll get kicked in the head."

They both laughed lightly, easily, and he reached across the table and took her hand. "Ali, it's really good to see you again."

She froze, her laughter dying abruptly as the feel of Jake's hand sent slivers of awareness through her. She didn't want to respond to him, didn't want to remember how wonderful it felt to have his hands on hers. That's not why either of them was here. Pulling away, she stood and started clearing the table.

Jake closed his eyes and took a deep breath.

*That's right, Jake, old buddy,* he thought. *Keep your distance, just like you planned.*

Feeling like a fool once again, he stood and started to help her, the strained politeness more unnerving than any argument. It didn't help that he was sharply aware of her as a woman, of her soft scent and the way the light caught and reflected off the strands of red in her hair. Her every move and gesture played havoc with his senses, and he had to remind himself over and over again that there was nothing between them except a lot of hard feelings and unanswered questions.

At last they finished cleaning up, and Jake escaped to tend the fire while Ali made coffee. He took his time building it up to a crackling blaze, not anxious for another encounter of any kind with his hostess. Just when he could no longer find anything else to do to make the fire burn brighter, she came into the room carrying a tray ladened with a coffeepot, mugs, sugar bowl and creamer.

Setting it on the table in front of the wraparound

couch, she said, "Would you like something stronger? I know Granddad has a bottle or two of brandy hidden around here somewhere."

Jake seriously considered it. A good strong shot of something more potent than coffee might be just what he needed. Then again, it might make matters worse. He was barely hanging on to his self-esteem as it was. Lord only knew how he'd manage to embarrass himself if he started drinking. "No thanks," he said. "Coffee's fine."

She nodded and filled the two mugs, putting one on a napkin and sliding it across the table toward him. "I'll let you fix your own since I don't know how you take it." Then she took the second mug and settled back on the couch, pulling her feet up and tucking them beneath her.

Jake picked up the mug she'd poured for him but didn't join her on the couch. Instead, he sipped at the hot coffee and retreated to stand once again in front of the fire. For several minutes he watched the bright orange-and-yellow flames rip at the wood, devouring it with a voracious appetite, and waited for her to start speaking. She'd promised to explain why she'd brought him here, and although he was beginning to get the picture all too clearly, he wanted to hear her say it. He considered himself a patient man, but he didn't think he could take another thirty-six hours of the kind of tension he'd experienced over the last two.

Finally, he could wait no longer. Setting the nearly full mug on the mantel, he turned and folded his arms across his chest, tucking his hands beneath his biceps. "Okay, Ali, it's time."

She looked up at him sharply, as if she'd forgotten he was there.

Before she could put him off again, he added, "I think we've danced around the real issue long enough. Now, tell me why I'm here."

For a moment she didn't answer, holding his gaze with eyes haunted by the firelight. Then she looked down, concentrating on the cup in her hand as if it had all the answers.

"Ali?" he prodded, moving away from the stone hearth to sit across from her on the couch.

She took a deep breath, as if bracing herself, and looked up at him. There was no anger in her eyes now, only a sadness that tugged at him, weakened his resolve to get everything out in the open.

But it was too late for that.

As little as a month ago, it would have been simpler to just let things alone. They'd both gone on with their lives and had attained a measure of contentment. Then she'd stirred things, opening up old wounds by bringing him to this cabin. Now they had no choice but to examine the past, dissect it and lay it wide open. Only then would they be able to put it behind them and get on with their lives.

Maybe it was for the best, but he sure as hell didn't have to like it.

"I brought you here to ask you a question," she said into the tense silence.

"Seems like a lot of trouble just for a question." He shrugged, though he knew this was where they needed to begin. "But go ahead, ask."

Again she hesitated, but briefly this time. "I want to know what happened twelve years ago. Why you left without a word, without..." Her voice broke, and he almost went to her, but she recovered quickly, and he managed to keep his distance and his self-respect for once. "Without saying goodbye."

Jake sighed. Now that it was out, he had to admit he'd known all along that this was her reason for bringing him here. He *owed* her an explanation. Maybe that's why he'd agreed to come, because he also needed to put an end to the wondering, to all the questions they'd left unanswered twelve years ago.

But how much of the truth could he tell her? How much was he willing to reveal? He decided to start with the obvious. "We never would have made it."

She arched an eyebrow, urging him to continue without saying a word.

He scooted forward, clasping his hands together and resting his elbows on his knees. "Look, Ali, you were a nice kid and all—"

"A nice kid?" Her voice snapped with irritation. "Is that how you thought of me?"

"Yes." It was his first almost-lie. She *had* been a nice kid, raised in a good home with family and friends who loved her. But then again, she'd been so much more to him. For a boy from the streets, she'd been everything good and light. Everything he could never be. At least he'd realized it before ruining her life.

But he couldn't tell her that.

Instead he said, "After I left the ranch, I wandered for months, living off the back of trucks and picking up odd jobs here and there. What kind of life would that have been for a girl like you?"

"A girl like me?"

He shrugged and glanced around the cabin. "You know, someone raised with all the advantages."

"You decided I couldn't live without all the things

I'd been used to?'' There was disbelief and accusation in her voice. ''Who were you to make that choice for me?''

''I was the only one *capable* of making a choice.''

She pulled back and the hurt in her eyes surprised him. After all these years he hadn't expected to be able to hurt her. Nor had he wanted to.

''Look,'' he said. ''I didn't say I was proud of it.'' He shifted uncomfortably on the couch, fighting the urge to rise and pace. ''But yeah, I made the choice, the only reasonable choice. It would have taken you less than six months to get fed up with that kind of life. And then you would have been on the phone to your daddy in Atlanta, who would have probably had me arrested for kidnapping or something.''

She shook her head. ''I don't believe this. What makes you so sure I wouldn't have been able to handle it?''

''Because I'd been there.'' He held her gaze, willing her to see the truth in his words. She was the only person he'd ever told about his life before he'd been sent to Lost Springs Ranch, about his first, nightmarish thirteen years. And about his mother. ''I'd lived on the streets and knew what it was like.''

Ali looked away abruptly, obviously uncomfortable with the memories. Jake understood. Hell, he hated thinking about that time, as well, but sometimes the ghosts gave him no choice.

But she recovered quickly and said, ''Let me see if I've got this straight.'' She lifted her eyes to his again, and the anger he'd seen in them earlier had returned. ''Basically, you left me before I could leave you.''

He flinched at the harshness in her voice and the

directness of her words. But he couldn't deny it, either. Nor could he make what he'd done sound noble, as if he'd left her for her own good. It had been a totally selfish act, and she'd hit it right on the head.

When he didn't respond, she obviously had her answer and said in a strained voice, "So, did you care at all? Or was I just convenient?"

Jake ran an unsteady hand through his hair. It would be so easy to tell her the truth, to tell her how much he *had* cared, that leaving her had been the hardest thing he'd ever done. But it was too late for that.

"Sure, I cared," he said with a shrug, brushing off the question as if it had no significance. "But, Ali, we were just kids...." As if that explained away what he'd felt—what they'd both felt—as unimportant.

"I see." Her eyes were dry, but he heard the hurt in her voice. He went to her side, but she shifted away before he could touch her. "So why didn't you just tell me instead of running off?"

He looked away, ashamed. About this at least, he'd give her the whole truth. "I didn't tell you because I couldn't face you. I was a coward." This time he gave in to the need for movement and rose to stand in front of the fireplace. Without looking at her he went on. "I was young and stupid. And for that, I apologize." He turned back to face her, the way he should have done twelve years ago. "I was wrong."

For several long minutes she didn't say anything, then she pushed herself stiffly off the couch. "Thank you for telling me the truth."

He wasn't worthy of her thanks. "Ali—"

"Let it go."

As little as an hour ago, that was what he'd wanted.

But now? He wasn't sure what he wanted or needed anymore.

"It's late," she said, before he could put voice to his thoughts. "And I'm tired. I'm going to go on to bed."

He took a deep breath and nodded. It was probably a good idea. It had been a long, tense evening, and they both could use a little time and space to sort things out.

"Good night," she said, and started toward the stairs.

Suddenly he couldn't let her go. Not yet. "Ali, wait." He crossed the room to her, stopping just short of touching distance.

She looked at him with wary eyes. "What is it?"

He took a step back and shoved his hands into his pockets, suddenly not knowing exactly what he'd wanted to say. "Nothing. I just wanted to..." He searched for something, anything to keep her here a moment longer. "Thanks for dinner."

She tilted her head slightly, and he could see she wasn't buying it.

*Oh, hell.*

"That's not true," he said. "There's one other thing." Closing the distance between them, he lifted his hand and ran the back of his fingers down her cheek. He heard her sharp intake of breath and saw her eyes widen.

"I owe you one more thing," he said, and taking the final step forward, he lowered his mouth and gently brushed his lips against hers.

She offered no resistance. But when he pulled back, she said, "What was that for?"

"It was the goodbye I should have given you twelve years ago."

Her eyes instantly filled with tears, and a band tightened around his heart. It was all the prodding he needed, and he raised his other hand to cradle her face in his palms.

"And this," he whispered as he once again lowered his mouth to hers, "is what I should have done the moment I arrived."

# CHAPTER FOUR

ALI KNEW SHE SHOULD STOP him, pull away before Jake's lips met hers again, but the one brief touch hadn't been enough. Not nearly enough. She wanted to feel his mouth on hers, wanted to explore the taste of him. Then he was kissing her, gently at first, before deepening his claim on her senses, and all thoughts of stopping him fled her mind.

She inched closer, her hands caught between them, her fingers splayed against his chest. He was both the boy she remembered and a man she'd just met. The feel of him was new, larger, stronger, more confident as he coaxed her mouth open and probed the depths within. But there was recognition, too—a pull within her that no other man had ever created. He was the boy she'd fallen in love with, the boy she'd given herself to body and soul, the boy who'd left her alone and pregnant.

As the thought struck her, she broke the kiss and tried to back away, but he didn't release her. Surprised, she met his dark eyes and lost herself once again. She tried to remember why she needed to get away from this man, why she shouldn't be standing in his arms and allowing him to kiss her. Instead, it was as if time stood still, as if they had no past or future. There was only now.

Of course that was silly, a fantasy best left to overly

imaginative seventeen-year-old girls. Taking a deep breath, she said, "This isn't a good idea."

He smiled. "No. I don't expect it is." Dropping his hands from her face, he circled her waist and pulled her closer. "But it never stopped us before."

Ali resisted for one quick heartbeat, then closed her eyes and rested her head against his shoulder. He was doing it again, drawing her in when she should be running the other way.

What was it about this man that made her lose her good sense?

She was a woman who prided herself on sound judgment and practicality, and once again Jake had managed to destroy both. That in itself should have had her pulling away from him. But she couldn't. Not yet. It had been so long since a man had held her, and even longer since she'd wanted a particular man's arms around her.

Finally, with obvious reluctance, Jake released her. It was all she needed to regain control and put some distance between them.

"Well, I'm tired," she said, embarrassed and a bit flustered, though determined not to show it. It was, after all, only a kiss. "I think I'll call it a night."

He nodded without speaking.

"Make yourself at home," she said. "And if you're up before me in the morning, help yourself to whatever you find in the kitchen."

"Thanks." He reached out to touch her again, but this time she managed to back up before he made contact. It had been a simple kiss, the goodbye they should have shared twelve years ago, and she wouldn't let it be more.

"Good night, Jake." She turned away quickly, before she could give in to temptation and fall back into his arms.

In her room, she closed the door and stood for a moment with her hand still on the knob, her head against the hard wood, wondering how things could get worse. Letting Jake kiss her had been a foolish thing to do. She'd brought him here to rid herself of her adolescent fantasies, not reenact them.

Drawing a deep breath, she wrapped her hands around her middle and turned to press her back against the door.

Lust.

There was no other explanation that made sense. And in all honesty, she'd been on shaky ground long before he'd kissed her. From the moment he'd arrived at the cabin, or maybe as far back as the day of the auction, she'd been physically aware of him. It had kept her skittish and off balance, and struggling to maintain her distance. But she hadn't understood how strongly she wanted him until he'd touched her. Add to that her few, disappointing sexual experiences with other men, and it was no wonder she was ready to throw herself into Jake's arms. Her memories of making love with him, like everything else, were distorted. Maybe she needed to disprove that misconception, as well.

She shook her head and laughed silently at her convoluted logic.

What a way to convince herself it was okay to desire Jake, and maybe to make love with him. After all, it couldn't be as good as she remembered, could it? And hey, why not find out for sure? She'd come this far; things couldn't possibly get worse.

Or could they?

Even if she succeeded in keeping her sexual urges under control, there were other problems with her plan. When Jake had explained his reasons for leaving her, she couldn't hate him as she'd wanted. She couldn't even sustain her anger. He'd been as honest and straightforward with his answers as she'd been with her questions. And what he'd said made sense— more sense than she would have admitted twelve years ago. She should at least be indignant that he'd made the choice for her, and a part of her was, but mostly she knew he was right. She'd said it herself a hundred times over the last twelve years: Jake had done her a favor by walking out on her.

Okay, so things weren't going exactly as she'd planned. The weekend wasn't over yet. After all, she still had to tell him about Sam. Several times during their conversation, Ali had almost told Jake about his daughter. But the moment had never seemed right. Besides, how did one go about breaking that kind of news to a man? She could just hear herself. "By the way, Jake, thought you might want to know I was pregnant when you left. And guess what? You have a daughter. She's eleven and looks just like you."

Ali knew that would go over really well.

Of course, that was just an excuse. When the time came, she'd have to say it. And depending on how he reacted, her plan would be back on track or seriously derailed. She actually considered going back out there and telling him now, but decided against it. With the memory of his kiss still fresh on her lips, she was afraid Sam wouldn't be on either of their minds. No, she needed to give herself a little time before facing him again.

She'd get a good night's rest and consider telling

him in the morning. After that she'd see what he wanted to do, whether he planned to get to know his daughter or not. She almost hoped he wouldn't ask to be a part of Sam's life—it would be easy then to put him behind her and maybe even dislike him. Then she felt guilty about the renegade thought. Sam deserved to know her father. If he made Ali uncomfortable, well, she'd just have to deal with it.

Sam came first.

With that decision firmly in mind, Ali climbed wearily into bed and burrowed deep beneath the heavy comforter. Still, sleep didn't come easily. She tossed and turned, no longer thinking about her plan and how it had failed, or about what might happen when Jake found out about Sam. Instead, Ali remembered his kiss; the feel of his mouth on hers. It had created an ache within her that she thought she'd never experience again. She wanted him, and all the logic she was so proud of never even entered the picture. He had the power to make her forget herself, to make her forget who and what she was.

And that frightened her more than anything.

JAKE KNEW HE WASN'T GOING to get much sleep. Not after that kiss.

Settling down on the couch in front of the fire, he leaned his head back against the pillows and closed his eyes.

Why had he done it?

He and Ali had talked things over and gotten everything out in the open. He should have been satisfied with that and let things be. Instead, he'd kissed her. For twelve years he'd struggled to put his memories of her aside, and with one brief touch of her lips, those years had melted away.

Cursing silently, he ran a hand down his face before dropping it once again to his lap.

He should have noticed when things began to shift between them and been on his guard. Looking back, he saw that the first softening had occurred when Ali started talking about her job. The tension between them had eased, and he'd gotten a glimpse of the woman she'd become. Not the edgy, angry woman who'd brought him to this cabin, but the warm, caring woman who'd chosen to tend sick animals for her life's work.

She'd accomplished so much, reaching for and fulfilling her dream. And it had changed her, made her stronger. Despite her obvious discomfort around him, there was a calmness and confidence in her that hadn't been there twelve years ago. As a girl she'd been headstrong, determined, sure of what she wanted. At least on the outside. Jake had known her better than most, and had always suspected that underneath the strong-willed teenager was a fragile and unsure girl. Not any longer. She'd come into her own, and he was proud of her and what she'd achieved.

Later, when she'd faced him and asked her questions, he'd again had to admire her courage and strength. She'd grown into a hell of a woman. And that's why he'd kissed her.

Or was it?

He couldn't say for certain whether that was the reason or not. He didn't know if it was his current attraction to this new and exciting woman, or the leftover love for the girl she'd once been. Or maybe it had been plain old lust. Lord knew it had been a while

since he'd been with a woman, and under the circumstances—alone in a mountain cabin with Ali—what
man wouldn't experience a twinge or two of sexual
desire.

So where did that leave him? Leave *them?*

It had been an impossible relationship twelve years
ago. They'd been kids from vastly different worlds on
a collision course with disaster. A lot had changed
since then. He and Ali had changed; they'd grown up.
Still, a lot about them had remained the same.

All Jake had to do was glance around the room to
recognize that.

There was money here. Not that the cabin was
flashy or luxurious; Austin Kendrick had been more
subtle than that. But there was an attention to detail
that didn't come cheaply. The high-grade oak floors
and staircase, the durable but attractive furniture, and
the small, efficiently designed kitchen with top-of-the-
line cabinets and appliances were just a few of the
niceties that made this a place Jake would never be
able to afford. Normally that wouldn't have mattered
to him. Except now, this cabin belonged to Ali. Call
it foolish male ego or antiquated chauvinism, but the
fact stared him harshly in the face.

There was nothing he could give Ali that she
couldn't get for herself.

Which brought him right back to where he'd been
twelve years ago. It didn't matter how much he
wanted Ali, they were still worlds apart. The difference now was that Jake wasn't going to allow his
physical urges to get in the way of his better judgment. Nor was he going to take off like he'd done as
a boy. He'd stick the weekend out, as he'd promised.
Then he'd be on his way.

Meanwhile, he just needed to keep his hands to himself and his hormones under control.

ALI AWOKE TO BRIGHT yellow sunshine and the smell of brewing coffee. She lay quietly for a moment, disoriented. Then the morning shifted into place and everything came back in a rush: Jake's arrival at her cabin yesterday, dinner, their awkward conversation.

The kiss.

She closed her eyes and a wave of disquiet settled in her stomach. The little sleep she'd gotten had done nothing to alleviate her distress at having to face Jake this morning. Between her determination to make her plan work and her resolve to avoid any more physical contact with him, she knew it was going to be a difficult day. Not to mention that at some point she still needed to tell him about Sam, a daunting task in itself.

Besides the rich aroma drifting up from her kitchen, there were the definite sounds of movement downstairs. She briefly considered staying in bed. If she knew Jake, it wouldn't be long before he headed outside. He never could take being indoors for long. Especially not on a bright summer day. She could wait him out and maybe wouldn't have to face him for a while. Hours, maybe. But that was the coward's way out, and she'd never been a coward.

Still, she took her time showering and dressing in a clean pair of jeans and T-shirt. She flirted with the idea of applying makeup but decided against it. It was the principle of the thing. Besides, she refused to prove Gail right. Ali wasn't going to try to make herself into something she wasn't just to impress Jake Merrill, no matter what her friend believed.

By the time she wandered out of her bedroom and

down the stairs to the kitchen, the smell of bacon had been added to that of coffee.

"Morning," he said, looking impossibly cheerful considering the previous evening. He'd evidently had no trouble sleeping last night—which irritated her. But what did she expect, she asked herself, that he'd lain awake half the night just as she had?

"Good morning," she answered, trying not to sound churlish.

"You look like you could use some coffee." Without waiting for her reply, he retrieved a mug from the cabinet and filled it. "I hope you don't mind that I made myself at home."

She took the cup from him and settled safely behind the kitchen table. "No, of course not."

"Good, because I woke up hungry." He returned to the stove and the pan of sizzling bacon, where he expertly turned one slice after another.

"I thought you didn't cook."

"Only breakfast. I worked roundup for a couple of seasons, and the first year they put me on morning detail. It was a small outfit that couldn't afford a full-time cook, so we all took turns. In my case, it was learn to feed a crew of hungry men or pay for it the rest of the day." He tossed her a grin over his shoulder. "They were merciless, and when I started, I couldn't so much as scramble an egg."

Ali smiled into her coffee at the image of a bunch of hard-bitten cowboys giving a much younger Jake a rough time. "So you learned to make breakfast."

"You better believe it. How do pecan pancakes sound?"

Ali winced. "Fattening. And I can't believe you found pecans in this kitchen."

"I dug around a bit." He shrugged, looking a bit embarrassed and entirely too handsome for so early in the morning. "There was an unopened can on a bottom shelf."

"I think I'll just have coffee."

He turned, cooking fork in hand, and gave her a mock frown. "You're afraid to try my pancakes?"

He presented such an incongruous image—this large man in faded denim, boots and a flannel shirt, cooking in her kitchen—she hardly knew how to respond. "No, I—"

"I ate your chili."

She shook her head, hoping to dispel the disturbing image of Jake making her breakfast. This was not the way to change her memories of him. "Pancakes and bacon. Too much fat and cholesterol for me."

He looked her over, and she felt his gaze as surely as if he'd run his hands over her. "Looks to me like you've hardly put on a pound since you were seventeen."

She laughed shortly. "Hardly." Pregnancy had taken its toll, but she wasn't about to point that out. Though maybe it was time she told him about Sam. "Look, Jake—"

"No excuses," he interrupted, turning back to the stove. "I'm going to take it personally if you won't try my pancakes. Besides, I'll work it off you."

She almost gagged on her coffee. "I beg your pardon?"

He removed several strips of bacon from the pan and laid them in neat rows on a paper towel. "I thought we could go hiking." He didn't bother to look at her but continued laboring over his breakfast preparations. "You still like to hike, don't you?"

She nodded uncertainly, still thrown by the image of the two of them working off an indulgent breakfast in a fashion that had nothing to do with a walk in the woods. "Occasionally."

"There must be some good trails around here."

"A few."

He fiddled with the frying bacon for a moment longer, retrieved his coffee and turned to lean against the counter. "So, what do you say?"

She just stared at him, not quite sure what to say. "I don't know."

"Did you have something else in mind for the day?" he asked. "Some work you need done around here or something? I'd be glad to help out."

"No…no work," she managed to reply. "I have a local handyman who pretty much takes care of the place." As for other plans, she hadn't really made any, which wasn't like her. What had she intended to do with him all weekend? It was just one more indication of how dangerous it was for her to be around him. It threw her totally off, to the point where she no longer knew herself. "I brought some paperwork with me," she said, trying to recover. "I thought I could spend a couple of hours catching up." When he didn't respond to that, she said, "I guess I could do that later."

"Good." He looked so pleased with himself, standing there with that little-boy grin of his—a grin so much like Sam's. Spontaneity. It was a trait Ali had sometimes envied in her daughter, though she'd attributed it to Sam's age. Now she realized Sam had inherited it from her father. "Then it's settled."

Ali felt anything but settled, though she couldn't come up with a single rational reason why they shouldn't go hiking. After all, she'd brought him to the mountains—what else was there for them to do? They couldn't hang around the cabin all day staring at each other.

Before she could respond, he said, "But first we eat." He turned back to the stove and removed the remaining bacon from the pan.

Ali sat there, a bit stunned. She wasn't sure she wanted to spend the day hiking with Jake. No, she corrected herself, that was a lie. The thought of a day in the mountains sounded wonderful. That was the problem. It wasn't exactly the best way to dispel her memories of him. She'd fallen in love with him in the back country of Wyoming. Going there again would hardly repair the damage she'd done to her peace of mind by bringing him here.

Finally he turned to face her again, leaning against the counter and folding his arms across his broad chest. "What's the matter, Ali? Do I scare you?"

The question hit home. Did he scare her? No, *he* wasn't the problem. "I just think it's better if we don't stir things up any more than we already have."

"By going hiking?" He looked entirely too smug. "You *are* afraid."

"I am *not* afraid of you, Jake Merrill." She let her irritation show in her voice.

"I didn't say you were afraid of me. It's yourself you're afraid of. Either that, or you're afraid you'll enjoy yourself."

She couldn't deny the truth. Nor would she admit it to him. Besides, there were more important things they needed to discuss. Like Sam. That would certainly put a damper on his urge to go hiking. "Look,

Jake.'' She set down her mug and rubbed at her temples. ''We need to talk.''

He shrugged. ''I thought that's what we were doing.''

''No, I mean seriously.''

Crossing the room, he placed a hand under her chin and tilted her face upward so she was forced to look at him. ''Ali, we talked last night. I don't know about you, but I'm about all talked out. Let's put it aside and enjoy ourselves today.''

She wanted to draw away from his hand, but she had all she could do just to ignore the feel of his fingers on her skin and say, ''There's something I have to tell you.''

''Later.'' Sitting down in the chair next to her, he took her hand. ''Look. We're friends, right?''

She nodded, though *friends* had never been the word she'd used to describe their relationship.

''We're here, and it's a gorgeous day.'' He gave her hand a quick squeeze. ''We need a break. Both of us.''

He must have sensed her vacillating because he grinned and said, ''Come on, Ali, we used to have so much fun together. Let's go hiking.''

She laughed shortly and shook her head. She had to admit the whole idea was tempting. She glanced out the kitchen window to the bright sunshine beyond. It was a beautiful day. How could she refuse? So they'd spend a few pleasant hours hiking; that didn't mean things had to go any further between them, or that she'd suddenly change her mind about him. Or trust him. Besides, maybe it would make it easier to tell him about Sam.

''Come on,'' he nudged again.

"All right," she said, letting her smile break through. "I'll go."

After all, it was a relatively safe way to spend the day.

JAKE STEPPED OUT onto the porch and found himself in a world of dazzling beauty.

Last night's rain had cleansed the earth and left the mountains alive and vibrant with color. The ground was a rich, moist brown, the forest a multitude of vivid greens, and the sky a clear, brilliant blue. He breathed deeply, taking in the clean, crisp air, and understood why Austin Kendrick had spent his last years here. The older man had picked his spot well, building his cabin amid the towering pines with the rugged peaks of the Laramie Mountains at its back. A man could live his entire life in a place like this and never want for a thing.

Except maybe someone to share it.

With a short, self-deprecating laugh, he thought of how he'd talked Ali into this outing. It seemed to him the safest way to spend the day. For both of them. He wasn't sure he could handle being in close quarters with her all day and still manage to keep his distance. Just that one brief touch in the kitchen had been a mistake. He could still feel the smooth skin of her cheek against his fingers and the fragile bones of her hand in his. It wouldn't take much for him to pull her back into his arms. And from there it was a short hop to meltdown.

The door opened behind him and she stepped outside.

Without turning, he motioned toward the downward slope of the hill and said, "Most people would have cut down those trees so they could see the creek.''

She moved up to the edge of the porch and leaned against the railing. "I never knew Granddad to do anything the way most people did.''

Jake chuckled. "That's one of the things I liked best about him.''

"He used to say that if he cleared the trees so he could see the water, he might be tempted to sit on the porch and watch it all day." She smiled. "This way he was forced to walk down the hill to enjoy it.''

Jake nodded. "Makes sense.''

"In a strange sort of way, I guess it does.''

They were silent for a few minutes. It was an easy, comfortable silence—the first since he'd arrived yesterday—and he knew he'd been right to talk her into hiking in the mountains. There was a healing power here, a magic with the capacity to help them put their past to rest. They both needed that.

"Do your parents come out here to visit you much?" he asked.

"They try and get out here once or twice a year. But Dad's company keeps him busy, so they don't always make it. We..." She hesitated, and though Jake wondered about it, he didn't question her. "I go back to Atlanta several times a year. Usually for the holidays.''

"Now, that's something I don't understand.''

She threw him a questioning look. "What?''

"How a man like your father, who was raised out here, could turn his back on this country." He made a sweeping gesture with his hand. "Just look at this place.''

"We all need different things in our lives.''

"I know you're right, but…" He shrugged.

"Dad took after my grandmother. She lasted less than two years in Lightning Creek before heading back to L.A."

"Well…" Jake looked at her and smiled. "I'm glad you took after your grandfather."

She blushed lightly and looked away. "My parents have been great. Without them…" She let her voice trail off for a moment and threw him a quick glance. "Well, I have a lot to thank them for."

He was about to ask her what she meant, but thought better of it. He and Ali didn't need to start exchanging confidences. They were simply two old friends who were going to spend a day together hiking before going their separate ways. He didn't want to turn it into anything more.

She obviously had the same thoughts because she seemed to force a smile. "You know," she said, "you should be grateful the whole world doesn't want to live out here, or it would get too crowded. Where would people like you and me live then?"

"You've got a point." He laughed and thought how young she looked, with her freshly scrubbed face and her hair pulled back. She needed nothing to enhance her natural beauty. There was an openness and honesty about her that had always appealed to him. Even as a teenager, he'd had no interest in the flashier members of the opposite sex. To him they'd been nothing more than window dressing for the guys who'd chased after them. He'd never felt the need to hang an ornament on his arm. Instead, he'd wanted— no, he admitted, looking back from an adult perspective—he'd needed a friend. Someone to laugh with and talk to, someone he could trust.

Ali had been that person. And he'd walked out on her.

A rush of shame swept through him, and he turned away to stare once again at the quiet forest beyond the clearing, searching for the peace he'd found moments earlier.

"Jake." There was a question in her voice. "What's wrong?"

Perceptive, too, he thought. She'd always been able to read him far too easily for comfort. "Nothing," he answered, trying to put a smile back in his voice. Then, noticing the folded map in her hand, he added, "Have you decided where we're going?"

She hesitated a moment. "We have a couple of choices." Handing him the map, she stepped closer and pointed to a circle drawn in black ink. "This is Granddad's property, right on the edge of the Medicine Bow National Forest." She moved her slender finger to a thin blue line that intersected the circle, but he had a hard time paying attention to her words. Instead he thought of how it would feel to have her fingers—all of them—running over him.

"If we follow the creek downstream a couple of miles," she was saying, "we'll run into LaBonte Creek." The blue line merged with a thicker blue line, and the scent of her, the delicate fragrance of shampoo and soap, made his head swim.

"From there, it's another couple of miles to the Curtis Gulch Campground, where we can either take the LaBonte Canyon or Curtis Gulch Trail." She backed up a bit, and he breathed a sigh of relief. "Both are nice hikes, but the canyon is spectacular this time of year."

"Sounds like a plan." In truth, he was only

vaguely aware of the details she'd just gone over. "How far is it?"

"It's a full day's hike. I'd say round trip it's about eight miles." She smiled a challenge. "Or if that's too much for you, we can turn around at the campground and come back."

"Too far?" Jake handed her the map. It was exactly what he needed to keep his wayward imagination in line. Lots of long, hard exercise. "Lead on."

Still smiling, Ali started toward the cabin door. "I figured we'd eat on the trail, so I made some sandwiches. It'll just take me a minute to load up."

"I'll be waiting." He leaned back against the roof support and crossed his arms. "Then we'll just see who runs out of energy first."

Okay, he thought, so spending the day together wasn't going to be as easy as he'd hoped. All she had to do was get close to him and his hormones went into overdrive. Somehow he was going to have to keep as far away from her as possible.

Shaking his head, he laughed silently and without humor. "Yeah, right."

ALI HURRIED BACK into the house, eager to put a little distance between her and Jake.

Her initial instincts had been right. This hike wasn't a good idea. Not if she was serious about purging Jake Merrill from her memories. She could hardly breathe when he stood beside her. How was she going to spend the whole day with him?

Unfortunately, she didn't have any other choice.

She couldn't tell him she'd changed her mind. He'd want to know why, and she could hardly admit how strongly he affected her, that he made her senses sing

by just being close. And even if she did come up with
a plausible excuse, she didn't have anything better to
suggest. Other than admitting defeat and sending Jake
on his way back to Colorado, she was stuck with him
for the next twenty-four hours. And she was stuck
with this hike. She was just going to have to make
the best of it.

A few minutes later she was back outside, where
Jake waited with a pack slung over one shoulder. He
looked large, male and competent, as if he could handle anything, and Ali felt a little thrill run through
her. Jake had always been good in the woods. He
seemed to have a natural affinity for wild places. But
the last time she'd ventured out with him, he'd been
little more than a boy, cocky and sure of himself, but
with limited knowledge or experience to back it up.
That had changed. There was nothing cocky about
him now, just a quiet confidence that spoke volumes
about how he'd spent the past twelve years.

"Ready?" he asked.

She nodded, unwilling to trust her voice.

They started off down the hill toward the creek.
Jake took the lead and Ali followed, trying to ignore
the sheer maleness of the man in front of her. Within
minutes, they were beneath the pungent canopy of
pines, where the temperature dropped several degrees
and their footsteps echoed quietly among the watching trees. When they reached the creek, Jake stopped
and Ali came up beside him.

The water ran swiftly, sparkling with the early-
morning sunlight and filled with the late spring runoff
from the mountains. On the far bank, clusters of Ja-
cob's ladder bloomed in shades of blue and purple,

their delicate trumpetlike blossoms reaching for the sun.

"Granddad loved it here," she said, grateful for the memory that took her mind off the man at her side. "He'd sit on that flat rock over there and work his wood."

"You miss him, don't you?"

Tears stung her eyes but she forced them back. "Yeah, I do." With a tight smile she motioned toward the trail. "Come on, let's go."

Jake struck off unerringly, heading upstream along the path beside the river.

They fell easily into their old pattern of relaxed silence, each absorbed with their own thoughts and the peace and solitude of the surrounding woods. Jake had once told her that what he liked best about her was her knack for quiet. She'd learned that from her grandfather, she supposed, who'd always said that in the mountains, people needed to learn to listen—to the trees, the wind and the heart of the universe.

Now, following Jake, she seemed to be seeing this path for the first time, though she'd been this way dozens of times with her grandfather before his death and later with Sam. Once she'd even brought Gail. Yet, there was a sense of familiarity, too, walking with Jake as they'd done years ago, investigating the world around them.

Suddenly, he held up his hand and stopped short. Obeying his silent command, Ali slowed. Reaching back, Jake took her hand and drew her up beside him while keeping his eyes on the far bank. Following his gaze, Ali caught her breath and smiled.

Upriver, about two hundred yards, stood a large bull elk at the water's edge. She recognized him immediately. He was a massive animal. Standing more than five foot at the shoulders and probably weighing close to a thousand pounds, he carried a full set of antlers that spanned nearly four feet. He was alert, his head held high as if sensing their presence. At one point he seemed to look right at them, then, dismissing them as a potential threat, he lowered his enormous head to drink from the cool, clear water.

"That's King Lear," she whispered. "He comes here every spring."

Jake glanced down at her, a smile tugging at his lips. "King Lear?"

"That's what Granddad called him because of his arrogance. Once he actually walked through the yard while Granddad was on the porch."

Grinning, Jake turned back to watch the bull. "That's right, old boy, you just go ahead and drink your fill. You know we're not going to bother you."

Finally, the animal finished and lifted his head. Again, he seemed to stare right at them, his obsidian eyes bold and challenging. Then he turned and faded into the surrounding brush.

Jake laughed softly and shook his head. "I can see why your grandfather carved him in wood."

Surprised, Ali said, "You noticed the carving?"

"How could I miss it? All of them are good, but the one of old Lear there, well, it's magnificent."

"Yes, it is." It pleased her that Jake recognized her grandfather's talent. She'd often tried to convince him to show his work, if not sell it. He'd smile and shake his head, saying, "I'm just an old man trying to keep my hands busy. Working the kinks out of my joints."

"Now," Jake said, pulling her out of her memories, "should I expect to run into the model for that wooden grizzly around here, as well?"

"Granddad assured me that he carved the bear from his imagination."

"Let's hope he wasn't pulling your leg." Jake smiled down at her, and she realized he still held her hand. Her heart picked up its pace, and for a moment she couldn't breathe.

"Ah, Ali," he whispered, and his eyes drifted over her face until they came to rest on her lips. He lifted his hand to her cheek and stroked her with the back of his fingers, sending shivers of pleasure down her spine. "How did I ever let you go?"

The question sent a chill straight through her.

Backing up, she jerked her hand from his. "You didn't have room in your life for a nice kid." She hadn't meant to sound so bitter, to reveal how much anger she felt over his words last night, but she couldn't seem to help herself. "Remember?"

## CHAPTER FIVE

JAKE BACKED UP, silently cursing himself for being a fool. Touching her again had been stupid, but hurting her again had been the last thing he wanted to do. "I'm sorry, Ali."

She looked as unsettled as he felt. "Forget it," she said, and started to turn away.

Suddenly it seemed important to make her see their past for what it was, the good as well as the bad. Maybe then they could both move on with some kind of future. "You *were* a nice kid," he insisted.

"Stop saying that."

"Why? It's the truth."

She scowled and crossed her arms. "So if I was such a nice kid, what were you?"

He thought about that for a moment, about all the adjectives that would have fit the teenage boy she'd known. Scared. Angry. Alone. "Stupid." *For leaving you.*

She held his gaze, her beautiful eyes searching his, and he felt her touch his soul. "No," she said, her expression softening. "You were a lot of things. But stupid wasn't one of them."

For a moment neither of them spoke, and something shifted between them. Jake couldn't say what, exactly, but it felt as if a piece of the barrier they'd built had fallen away. It wasn't what he wanted, what either of them wanted. But it seemed fate had her own plans for the two of them.

He nodded toward the trail. "We should get going." With that, he turned and started off again, following the creek upstream, lost in thoughts of the inevitable.

Like wanting Ali.

At first he'd tried to deny it, then tried to ignore it. But when she'd looked up at him with those big coppery-brown eyes of hers, he'd become sharply aware of her hand in his and the feel of her soft skin under his callused fingers. And her scent. For a moment, he'd forgotten himself and his vow not to touch her again. He'd been about to kiss her when he'd opened his mouth and said the first thing that came into his mind, the question that had been teasing at the edges of his consciousness since the day of the auction.

*Why had he left her?*

Even knowing the answer didn't help. Not when he was around her.

They walked the rest of the way to the Curtis Gulch Campground in silence. Then, since it was still before noon, they decided to go on for a while longer before stopping to eat. Also, after the solitude of the trail, the few families who'd set up camp seemed like entirely too many people. So they headed east along the LaBonte Canyon Trail.

Ali had been right. The canyon was breathtaking.

As the trail led them deeper into the gorge, the surroundings alternated between dense pine and cottonwood forests and meadows carpeted with red, yellow, white and pink wildflowers. Everywhere they looked were picturesque rock formations and abundant wildlife. They saw more elk, several cows with their throng of young, and a herd of bighorn sheep as they migrated toward the higher elevations. And there were smaller animals, as well—jackrabbits, prairie dogs, red squirrels and wild turkey.

The trail crisscrossed back and forth across the LaBonte Creek, taking them first along the south side, then to the rockier and more rugged north side.

As they came up on one particularly tricky crossing, Jake stopped and examined the best way to avoid ending up in the water. Not that it was dangerous. The span was fairly narrow, only three steps across on foot-sized rocks that jutted above knee-deep water. But the creek was running fast and hard, keeping the stones damp, moss-covered and probably slippery. One false step and it would be a long, wet walk home. He picked his way across carefully, then turned to offer Ali his hand.

She hesitated, and he didn't blame her. Since he'd almost kissed her the last time she took his hand, it was probably safest to avoid any further physical contact. But the rocks were slick, and she evidently didn't feel like a quick dip in the chilly water. With obvious reluctance, she took his offered hand, using him for balance as she started across.

She almost made it, too. Except fate once again stuck her nose into things.

Ali's foot slipped, and before either of them could breathe, Jake had an arm wrapped around her waist, stopping her fall and lifting her the last couple of feet to solid ground. For a moment, neither of them moved, their bodies flush against each other. A familiar warmth crept through him, and he watched as her eyes widened.

Then, as one, they sprang apart.

"I'm sorry..." he began.

"No, uh, it was my fault." Her hands fluttered nervously, brushing at her hair before wrapping themselves around her waist. "Thanks for keeping me from falling."

He felt as flustered as she looked. "You're welcome."

"I think we should go." Her hands came away from her waist and motioned toward the trail. Then, without waiting for his reply, she turned and started off again, taking the lead this time.

Walking behind her made things worse. Jake couldn't avoid watching the sway of her hips and the way her jeans hugged her bottom. No, she wasn't as thin as she'd been at seventeen. Her figure was fuller, more womanly, and if possible, even more tempting than it had been years ago. Damn, this whole day was turning into one long test of self-control—a test he was pretty damn close to failing.

They finally stopped to eat in a lush meadow dotted with yellow wallflowers and bright red Indian paintbrush. Finding a spot away from the trail with a sweeping view of the canyon, they sat with their backs against a large granite boulder while keeping ample space between them. Ali had brought thick ham and cheese sandwiches, apples and a couple of large bottles of water. They ate in silence, while a gentle breeze rippled through the tall grass and great white clouds cast moving shadows across the mountains.

After finishing his sandwich, Jake lay back in the grass with his hands under his head. It had been years since he'd felt content to laze away a sunny afternoon in a mountain meadow. When he and Ali had been together, they'd often spent long hours doing just that, lying side by side on a blanket they'd spread on the ground. Only then, they'd had more on their minds than taking in the scenery. They'd been obsessed with each other, and the solitude of the hills and forests allowed them to explore that obsession.

"Do you remember the time we ran into the black bear?" she asked quietly, as if reading his thoughts.

Jake smiled, despite the feeling that taking a trip down memory lane wasn't the smartest move. "How could I forget?" He and Ali had gone to Glenrock on an errand for her grandfather and decided to make a day of it. After buying lunch at a chain sub shop in town, they'd driven into the mountains for a picnic. He laughed softly, though at the time, it had been far from funny. "I thought we were dead."

"Really?" She smiled down at him, an element of surprise in her eyes. "You seemed so calm at the time."

"I faked it." As usual, they'd found a pretty spot off the road for lunch and a little time alone. They'd just unwrapped their food when the biggest bear Jake had ever seen ambled out of the brush about a dozen yards from them. At first, all three of them froze. Then Jake came to his senses. Figuring it had to be the smell of the spicy meatballs that attracted the animal, he grabbed both sandwiches and tossed them as far as he could in the beast's direction. Fortunately the bear was more interested in the food than the two teenagers. Later, in the safety of their borrowed truck, he and Ali had laughed nervously all the way back to Lightning Creek.

"Do you know how crazy that was?" he asked. "No one had any idea where we were. Anything could have happened, and they wouldn't have found us for days. Or even months.''

She smiled and rested her chin on her knees. ''Spoken like a true adult.''

''Yeah.'' He settled back to stare at the endless blue sky and thought how things had changed. Nowadays he gave lectures to groups of teenagers about taking off into the mountains without letting someone know where they were headed. ''Like an adult who's had to find kids who've done crazy things like we used to do.''

''Yeah, it was a little nuts. But at the time...'' She didn't finish her sentence and didn't need to. Jake knew what she meant. At the time, the woods were the only place they could be alone. And the last thing that had ever crossed their minds was safety.

They were venturing into dangerous territory here, dredging up old memories and the wealth of emotions that accompanied them.

''Tell me about your job,'' she said, changing the subject abruptly.

He glanced over at her, then settled back to watch the sky again just as a flock of geese flew by, heading straight north in perfect formation. It was safer than looking at her. ''There's not much to tell. I spend a lot of my time giving lectures and seminars on wilderness safety.''

''And the rescue work?''

''Most of the time there's very little to do.''

''And the rest of the time?''

''You fight the fear.'' He hesitated a moment. ''You're afraid you won't find whoever's lost. Or that when you do find them, it'll be too late. And the families..." He let his voice trail off, then took a deep breath. "Dealing with the families is the worst."

"It must be hard."

He nodded slightly. "It can be tough." Then, almost as an afterthought or because something within drove him to be totally honest with her, he said, "There's always the fear that you'll get caught in the same storm, avalanche or rock slide as the people you're looking for." Despite his usual claims to the contrary, working on a rescue squad was inherently dangerous. No matter how well trained or experienced the team, there was always the fear that this time you might not return.

After a moment of silence, she asked, "So why do you do it?"

"Well, I like the solitude," he answered. "And the mountains."

Her expression softened, and for a few seconds he felt as he had earlier, lost in her wondrous autumn-colored eyes. They seemed to look right through him, into the depths of his soul where all his secrets were hidden. Something tightened in his chest, and he realized how much this woman still meant to him. He'd been fooling himself when he thought it was all in the past.

"But that's not why you do it," she said, drawing him out of his thoughts. "It's not the mountains or solitude, is it? Not really."

He couldn't be anything but totally honest. "There are the times when everything works out. You pull a survivor out of a coffin of snow, or find a toddler who wandered too far from camp, and, well..." He took a deep breath and pressed his lips together. "That makes all the difference. It makes the times you fail somehow easier to take.''

She held his gaze for a moment longer, as if searching for the truth behind his words. Finally she nodded and looked away, and he had the feeling that she understood.

Turning on his side, he rose up on one elbow and watched her. She sat with her back against the boulder, her eyes closed and face lifted to the sun, which caught and reflected off the strands of red in her hair. She was beautiful, intelligent and compassionate. He couldn't help but wonder why some other man hadn't claimed her for his own.

''So how come you never got married?'' he asked.

She glanced sideways at him with a slight frown. ''What makes you so sure I didn't? I could be divorced.''

''Are you?'' Without planning to, he reached up and tucked a stray strand of hair behind her ear. ''Divorced, that is.''

She looked away, a slight blush touching her cheeks, and he jerked his hand back. She wasn't nearly as unaffected by him as she wanted him to believe. ''No, I'm not divorced. I've never been married.''

He smiled to himself, pleased—though he'd given up the right years ago to feel anything one way or the other about her marital status. ''Ever come close?''

''Not really.''

''Why not?''

''My, we are getting personal here, aren't we?'' There was an edge to her voice, and again he smiled. It was okay for her to delve into his secrets, but not the other way around. Especially when it concerned the topic of love or marriage.

"It's an innocent-enough question between old friends," he countered.

"Is it?" She finally looked at him again. "Then what about you? Ever been married or almost married?"

He shrugged. "I came close once."

"Really?" She seemed a little taken aback by that, and he wondered if it was jealousy he saw in her eyes. "What happened?"

He settled back on his arms and plucked at the long grass beneath one hand. "We went our separate ways before we made a big mistake."

"Did you leave her, too?"

"Boy…" He glanced back at her and grinned. "You're really good at the potshots."

She looked at him without apology. "You started this conversation."

"You're right. And no, Janie walked out on me." She'd accused him of being cold and distant. At the time he'd convinced himself it wasn't true, that she was spoiled and demanding. Now he knew she'd been right. "I was a jerk, I guess."

He almost expected Ali to agree with that assessment. Instead she surprised him by asking, "Did you love her?"

He hesitated, thinking about her question and the best way to phrase his reply. "I thought I did." Looking back, he'd been more angry than hurt when Janie left him. Just when he thought he'd finally broken Ali Kendrick's hold on him, things had fallen apart. He'd been unable to give himself to Janie, or any other woman, because Ali had always been there. In his dreams. In his thoughts. And in his heart. Somehow, he didn't think he could explain that to her. Instead, he said, "When it was all over, I was more relieved than anything. It wouldn't have been fair to her if we'd gotten married."

"Why not?"

He looked at her, considering how she'd respond to the truth. Deciding not to risk it, he said, "You don't really want me to answer that, do you, Ali?"

For a moment she didn't reply, then she turned away. "I guess not."

They fell back into silence. Ali wrapped her arms around her knees and again closed her eyes and lifted her face to the sun. Jake continued to watch her, still wondering why no man had claimed her.

"You know," he said. "You didn't answer my question."

"Which question?"

"Why you never came close to getting married."

She sighed. "Too busy, I guess."

He didn't buy that—maybe wishful thinking on his part—but he decided to let it go. A part of him wanted to believe her feelings for him had been the cause of her not marrying, just as the memory of her had stopped him from loving again. Yet, he knew that was selfish and unreasonable. Ali deserved to be happy, even if that meant loving and marrying someone else.

"Do you remember the time we went up to Devil's Tower?" he asked.

She hesitated before answering. "Vaguely."

He grinned. She'd never been a very good liar. In this case he knew all too well why she was pretending not to remember. As if to jog her memory, he said, "You told your grandfather that you were spending the night with Gail. And I was supposed to be running errands for the Duncans.''

"I seem to remember something like that,'' she hedged, her flushed cheeks giving her away.

"We spent the day exploring the park around the tower. Afterward we drove farther north a bit and set up camp near a stream.'' He frowned, as if trying to recall something important. "What was the name of it?''

"Beaver Creek,'' she said, then glanced at him quickly, obviously embarrassed that he'd caught her remembering the incident. "I've spent a lot of time in the area since,'' she added in explanation.

"Have you?'' He sat up and shifted closer to her, even while his common sense told him to back off and not touch her. Ignoring the warning, he reached over and ran the back of his fingers down her cheek.

She blushed again, and he said, "Do you remember going swimming?'' He lowered his voice, feeling the memories wrap around them. "It was almost sunset, and there was no one else around. We were both pretty grubby from hiking all day, and neither of us had a swimsuit with us.'' She trembled, and he brushed her bottom lip with the pad of his thumb. "And the water was icy cold.''

"Jake…''

"Shh.'' He turned her face to his, knowing he was setting them both up for a fall if he didn't stop this. But he couldn't, not with her sitting so close, with the fragrance of her drifting around him.

"Don't fight it,'' he said, to himself as well as her. He dropped his gaze to her lips. Soft and moist, they begged to be kissed—though she'd never admit it. "I want to kiss you, Ali. I know it's not a good idea.

Not for either of us.'' He lifted his eyes to look into hers and saw her struggle. God, how he wanted her, how he'd always wanted her. ''Say yes, anyway.''

For a moment she reminded him of a frightened doe, cornered and looking for a way out. He caressed her neck, soothing her as she would one of her patients. Then she sighed, closed her eyes briefly and tilted her head toward his. It was all the answer, all the encouragement he needed. Sliding his hand to the back of her head, he pulled her to him until her mouth belonged to him.

Last night, the kiss had been an impulse, a tentative exploration that neither of them had planned or expected. Even the second, deeper kiss had been ambivalent. But this time there was nothing hesitant on either of their parts. She opened to him eagerly, answering his demands with her own as he lowered her to the grass.

A part of him whispered that this was crazy, that no good would come of the two of them getting involved again. But he silenced the voice, giving over instead to the woman, to the feel of her slender body beneath his, the honeyed taste of her mouth and the sweet sensation of total rightness.

Breaking away for a moment, he stared into her eyes. They were dark and hungry, and he felt an answering need within himself. ''God, I've missed you, Ali.''

She smiled and moved her hands to frame his face. ''I've missed you, too.'' Then, slipping her arms around his neck, she drew him back down. He found her mouth again, restless and greedy, with a heat that was more than he'd expected, more than he remembered. It was like a burst of sunlight on a cloudy day, and he knew with blinding clarity that he'd never stopped loving this woman.

Ali wondered how she'd lived so long without this man and his mouth doing delicious things to hers. She didn't remember wanting him so badly, needing him, but her body remembered and responded ravenously.

She felt wicked and wanted, and loved every minute of it.

Then his fingers brushed against her skin as he pulled her T-shirt from the waistband of her jeans, and a fresh, urgent wave of desire swept over her. Moaning, she arched against him, begging him without words to touch her. He answered instantly, sliding his hands beneath the thin cotton fabric. Never had she hated female clothing more than when he cupped her breast through her bra. She wanted to feel skin against skin.

He seemed to read her mind, because he found the front closure of her bra, unfastened it and pushed it aside. His fingers were both rough and gentle at the same time, teasing her nipples until they ached beneath his touch. Tightening her hold on him, she moaned softly into his mouth and moved into his caress.

"Ali," he whispered, his voice sounding strained. "We shouldn't do this. Not here. Not now."

"No, we shouldn't," she agreed, though her body seemed to have a mind of its own. Lifting her leg to rub her thigh against him, she felt his instant response and laughed silently, pleased with the feminine power she held over him.

No matter what else happened, right now he wanted her.

"If you don't stop that—" his voice was almost a

groan "—it won't matter what we should or shouldn't do."

"What about you?" His fingers still toyed with her breast, and she lifted her head to nibble at his mouth. "Do you expect me to stop with your hand inside my shirt?"

He smiled and lowered his head to rest against hers. "But you feel so good." He cupped one breast before moving to the other and nuzzling her ear. "*This* feels so good."

She couldn't argue with him. The gentle tug of his fingers sent swirls of pleasure throughout her, making it difficult to think.

Then with a sigh, he withdrew his hand from beneath her shirt and, after one final brief kiss, rolled off her. For a minute or two, neither of them moved. Finally, Ali took a deep breath and sat up. With her back to him, she reached beneath her T-shirt and fastened her bra.

"I have the feeling that may have been the stupidest thing I've ever done," he said in a hoarse drawl.

"What, kissing me?" She knew the feeling. Stupid but wonderful.

"No, stopping."

She glanced back at him and couldn't help but laugh. He looked in bad shape, lying on his back with an arm thrown across his eyes, the evidence of what they'd almost done still obvious by the bulge in his jeans.

He dropped his arm and smiled. Then he pushed up to sit next to her. She thought he'd kiss her again and was disappointed when he merely toyed with a strand of her hair, wrapping it around his finger while lowering only his gaze to her mouth. "This isn't over, Ali. Not nearly over."

She felt herself caught by his words, by their implicit promise, and for a moment could hardly draw a breath. Then she mentally shook herself. Shifting away from him, she pulled her hair back into a neat ponytail and packed up the remains of their lunch.

"We better get back," she said when she could speak again. "It's getting late, and we have a long walk."

THEY HIKED BACK to the cabin in silence.

Ali felt weak-kneed and fuzzy-brained, oddly exhilarated and strangely deflated. It made no sense that she should feel all those things at once. Still, she did, and all because she and Jake had almost made love in a mountain meadow. The situation was absurd. They'd behaved just like the eager teenagers they'd once been. The only difference was, back then, they wouldn't have stopped. She told herself to be grateful that at least some things had changed. After all, she'd barely escaped what would have been a big mistake. But that's not how it felt. It felt as if she'd missed something, that she'd held something wonderful in her grasp and let it go.

Which was the most ridiculous notion she'd come up with yet.

Hadn't she decided just last night that Jake wasn't to be trusted? That no matter how appealing she found the thought of making love to him, she needed to keep her distance. He was dangerous to her peace of mind, and the last thing she needed was to make things worse by getting into a physical relationship with him.

So why had she let him kiss her again?

That was a stupid question if she'd ever asked one. She'd wanted him to kiss her. And more. She *still* felt the pull, the ache to reach out and touch him. The real question was, what now?

Although he'd warned her that this wasn't over, she knew the final decision would be hers. What did she want to happen when they got back to the cabin? No. The answer to that one was easy. The harder question was, what was she going to allow to happen? In one sense, she wished they'd finished what they'd started in the meadow. It would have saved her the trouble of going through the agony of making the decision once again.

She laughed silently and without humor at herself.

No one who knew her would ever believe the way she was behaving, or her absolute inability to think rationally when it came to Jake Merrill. Usually, when faced with a difficult decision, Ali made a list. A column for all the arguments for one side of a question, another column for the opposite side. In the end, the right decision was always simple and clear. Not this time.

On the negative side was one word that seemed to encompass a whole series of reasons why she should pack her bags and head home as soon as they got back to the cabin. *Trust.* She couldn't trust Jake. She'd given herself to him body and soul once before, and he'd walked out, leaving her alone and hurting. That wasn't something you forgot, not even after twelve years.

Then there was Sam.

No matter what happened tonight, chances were Ali would have to deal with Jake again because of their daughter. Some part of her still recognized that he might not want anything to do with Sam, but in her heart, Ali knew Jake was going to want to get to know his daughter. That wasn't going to be easy on Ali, and making love with him would only make it more difficult.

Without going any further to consider the complications of disease or pregnancy, she should be able to make her decision easily enough. There was no way she should even be contemplating making love with Jake tonight.

The problem was, she wanted him.

As strongly or more than she had when she was seventeen. Only now she understood that she might never feel this way about another man, and she wanted to find out if making love to Jake was as wonderful as she remembered. But most of all, she simply wanted him. It was as if some renegade part of her mind was conspiring against her common sense.

When they finally arrived back at the cabin, the sun sat atop the western mountains, turning the sky a soft gold. In minutes it would fade to gentle pinks and purples. Ali removed her pack, dropped it on the porch and collapsed on the top step.

Jake joined her. "Well, you were right," he said. "That was one heck of a hike." It was the first either of them had spoken since leaving the meadow, and obviously an attempt to break the silence without bringing up the subject that was on both of their minds.

Going along with him, she asked, "Are you hungry?"

He grinned, and she realized that was the wrong

thing to ask under the circumstances. Ignoring his silly smile and the heat in her cheeks, she continued. "I have a couple of steaks I brought up from town yesterday. Or there's a small pub with great hamburgers down the mountain a bit. We could go there if you prefer."

He reached over and took her hand. "Let's stay in, Ali."

It seemed foolish at this point to pull away her hand, but she did. "Okay."

"That is, if you don't mind." She heard the question in his voice, and it had nothing to do with dinner.

"That's fine," she answered. "I'll get cleaned up and throw on the steaks."

"There's no hurry. I'd like to get cleaned up, too." Something in his voice made her look at him. He was smiling, a soft, gentle smile that made her want to melt against him right there and then. She wondered if he did that on purpose, knowing the effect it had on her.

"Well, I guess I better get started, then." Standing, she grabbed her bag. "If you get finished before me, help yourself to whatever you find in the kitchen. There's snack food in the refrigerator—cheese, crackers, that sort of thing."

"Sounds good," he answered.

She started toward the door, but stopped when he said, "Do you want to talk about this, Ali?" She glanced back at him, and he added, "Do you want to talk about what happened today?"

"I don't know," she replied honestly. "Is there anything to say?"

He shook his head. "I'm not sure. I didn't plan it, if that makes you feel any better."

"No." She wrapped her arms around her middle. "I don't think either of us planned it." But it didn't surprise them, either. They both had known it could happen.

He studied her for several long moments. "Do you want me to leave? Go back to Colorado? I will, if that's what you want."

She couldn't answer him, not right away. Common sense told her to send him on his way, while her heart wanted him to stay. As she'd done twelve years ago, she went with her heart.

"No, Jake," she said. "I don't want you to leave."

# CHAPTER SIX

ALI TOOK HER TIME in the shower.

Instead of jeans, she pulled on a pair of slacks and a cream-colored cashmere sweater her mother had given her for Christmas. Ali hadn't worn the sweater since she and Sam had returned from Atlanta after the holidays. She felt it was too expensive and dressy for normal ranch wear, but somehow it felt right tonight. Soft and feminine. She also let her hair hang loose and applied the makeup she seldom used.

When she was done, she stood in front of her dresser mirror wondering if she was crazy. She couldn't fool herself about her reasons for taking extra time and effort with her appearance.

She wanted to look good, and she wanted Jake to notice.

A few minutes later she stepped out of the bedroom and paused on the balcony overlooking the great room. Jake had built a fire, and shadows flickered and danced on the walls. For a moment she watched him, her hands tight on the railing. He fussed with the fire, arranging wood and making sure each piece was in position to burn properly. Ali smiled. Like her grandfather, Jake couldn't just build a fire and leave it alone. He had to poke and prod until he was satisfied it was perfect.

Though she didn't make a sound, he must have

sensed her. Looking up, he met her gaze, and the room seemed all at once too warm. In the firelight, he was all masculine angles and dark shadows, and she sensed that if she joined him in front of that fire, there would be no resisting him. She would be deciding to make love with him by the mere fact of walking down those stairs.

She silently laughed at herself. Who was she kidding?

She'd made her decision when she'd asked him to stay and proceeded to dress in clothes she seldom wore and apply makeup she rarely used. Or even earlier, when she'd allowed him to kiss her this afternoon, and the past had become tangled with the present. She would have made love to him then, and all her posturing and questioning since was nothing more than self-delusion. No matter how many arguments she came up with to the contrary, she wanted to make love to Jake Merrill again. At least this once.

He turned to replace the fire screen, then rose and looked back at her. "Come down, Ali." Although he spoke in little more than a whisper, she heard every word. "Nothing's going to happen that you don't want."

Of course, that was the problem. Despite all the reasons why she shouldn't let things go any further between them, she wanted the same thing he did. She longed to pick up where they'd left off this afternoon, to experience the physical sensations she'd known only one other time in her life. She needed to make love to Jake and see for herself if it was as wonderful as she remembered.

Without consciously making a decision to do so, she turned toward the stairs and started walking. She held on to the smooth wooden railing as if it were a lifeline, or a means of escape if she finally came to her senses.

He met her at the bottom and took her free hand. With a smile, he said, "You look really nice."

She smiled in return. "Thank you."

"Come on." He tucked her hand beneath his arm and led her to the couch in front of the fire. "I've opened a bottle of wine."

On the coffee table sat a tray with wine, an ice bucket and two glasses. Releasing her, he retrieved the bottle from the ice. "I found this in the back of your refrigerator. I hope you don't mind that I opened it."

"No, of course not." It had been there for nearly a year, left over from the last time she and Gail had come up to the cabin with the kids. After putting the younger set to bed, the two women had shared one of the bottles of wine they'd brought with them. It had been an evening of confided secrets, giggles mixed with tears, and friendship. They'd gone to bed a little tipsy, never getting to the second bottle.

Jake filled both wineglasses and handed her one. Then, holding his glass up to hers, he said, "What shall we toast to? Memories or reunions?"

She met his gaze for a moment, her wineglass held aloft. "Memories, I think. The good and the bad."

Jake's smile broadened and he touched his glass to hers. "To memories."

She moved away from him, sipping her wine as she headed toward the fire, which was the only light in the room. "How hungry are you?" she asked.

"Starved."

She turned to look at him with an amused smile.

Although she knew he wasn't referring to food, she said, "Let's start with something light." Taking another sip of the wine, she turned toward the kitchen. "I have cheese and—"

He snagged her arm before she'd taken more than three steps. "I wasn't talking about food."

"Really?" she said, feigning innocence.

"Let me show you what I want." Setting down his glass, he stepped behind her and slipped an arm around her waist. Then he lifted her hair and nuzzled her neck. Shivering, she closed her eyes and barely suppressed a moan. He planted more gentle kisses along the highly sensitive skin, working his way downward, then pushed aside her sweater and continued his assault on her shoulder.

"Jake…" This time she let the soft sound of pleasure escape. Then her practical side surfaced. "Jake, I don't have anything…" Her cheeks heated at just the thought. "I mean, I'm not on the pill or anything."

"Don't worry. I'll protect you." Moving back up her neck, he whispered in her ear. "I'm not going to lie or play games, Ali. I want to make love to you."

Before she could respond, he turned her around and framed her face with his hands and kissed her softly. She trembled and clutched at his shirt with her free hand.

"I've been thinking of nothing else for weeks," he said against her mouth.

She opened her eyes and looked into his dark eyes—eyes so much like Sam's, like the daughter they'd made together the last time she'd given in to her desire for him.

"Since the auction," he said, gently kissing first

one edge of her mouth and then the other. "Awake or asleep, I've dreamed about you." Again he brushed her lips, first with his mouth, then with the lightest touch of his tongue. "About this."

*So have I,* Ali thought.

She couldn't say it aloud, though, and didn't know if she believed his claims. Jake had always known the right words to say, the right ways to touch her to make her want him. Twelve years ago when he'd talked her into his bed, she'd been a virgin, young, innocent, trusting. She was no longer any of those things, but it didn't lessen his ability to speak the right words, or her desire to believe him.

She backed away, only a couple of inches, but enough to give her breathing space and a moment to think. "What, aren't there any women in Colorado?" She put a teasing note into her voice so he wouldn't know how strongly he affected her.

"Oh, there's lots of women, all right." He brought his hand lower to brush the pad of his thumb against her lips, then took her glass from her and set it on the table next to his. "Just not you."

She laughed lightly, telling him without words that she wasn't buying his line for one moment. Though she wanted to. Lord knew, she wanted to.

A flicker of a frown flashed in his eyes, but then it vanished, and he smiled. "So you don't believe me." He lifted his other hand to cradle her face, and desire, warm and moist, coiled within her. "I guess I'll just have to prove it, then."

He kissed her as he had that afternoon, hot and hard, staking a claim on more than her mouth. With a soft moan she yielded to him and raised a hand to press against his chest. Hard male muscle teased her fingers, and she longed to tear aside the fabric that kept her from touching his skin.

What difference did it make whether he was telling the truth about wanting her these past weeks, or whether he was making it up as he went along? No other man had ever made her ache like this, and she no longer had the strength or will to fight it.

With that thought, impatience took hold of her, and she pulled at the buttons of his shirt, fumbling and popping several before she accomplished her goal. His skin was warm and firm, and his heartbeat quickened beneath her probing fingers. It was his turn to groan, a dark, primitive sound that roused a fresh wave of longing deep in her belly. She edged closer, and he took hold of her waist, drawing her hips forward until their lower bodies pressed together.

The feel of him, hard and ready, sent her already mounting desire spiraling higher. She lifted her hands to his open shirt and shoved it off his shoulders. They separated just long enough to rid him of the garment before coming back together eagerly, body to body, mouth to mouth, as if neither of them would ever get enough.

Jake devoured her mouth, while moving his hands restlessly over her, relearning the feel of her—the narrowness of her waist, the soft swell of her hips, the round hardness of her bottom. Then he pulled her closer until he felt, rather than heard, her soft moan of frustration. She felt so good. So incredibly warm and willing.

He broke the kiss to look into her eyes. They were half-closed and cloudy with passion. God, she was sweet. It had been too long since he'd wanted a woman this badly. Hell, he'd never wanted a woman the way he'd always wanted Ali.

Slipping his hands to the bottom of her sweater, he pulled it up over her head and tossed it aside. She went for the front clasp of her bra, but he stopped her. He wanted to see her this way first, all soft and sexy, her creamy breasts framed by a tiny bit of silk and lace and her nipples pebbled within their restraints.

He couldn't resist. Bending to one beaded nub, he took it and the fabric into his mouth and felt her fingers dig into his shoulders. Though he thought he'd explode from wanting her, he held back, nibbling with his teeth where before he'd simply sucked. He heard her sigh of pleasure as she let her head fall back and arched her back.

Jake grabbed her waist, holding her close as he continued his assault with his mouth. When he could wait no longer for the taste of her skin, he raised his head to kiss her while unhooking the clasp of her bra and pushing the silky fabric aside. Her breasts spilled into his hands, warm and full with passion-hardened nipples.

He backed away slightly to look at her.

She was still delicately formed, but fuller and more womanly than she'd been years ago. Her skin was the color and texture of cream, though he knew it would tan to a shade closer to cream-laced coffee in the summer sun. Her nipples were shades darker, a dusky rose, and tempting. So very tempting.

He bent to first one, then the other, taking them in his mouth while her hands kneaded his scalp. He didn't think he could get any harder, but the taste of her skin was an aphrodisiac that sent a fresh rush of blood straight to his groin.

It was time. They'd waited long enough, twelve years long enough.

Taking her hand, he led her to the couch and drew her back into his arms. He pressed the full length of his body against hers, kissing her thoroughly and deeply. Together they melted onto the sofa, and he edged a leg between her thighs. A moment, or an hour later, he lifted up on his elbows to gaze into her smoldering eyes. She was everything he remembered and more, woman and girl, sweetness and heat. Making love to her had become more essential than he'd ever thought possible.

He nipped at her mouth gently, once, twice, then pulled back to look at her once more. She smiled temptingly and dropped her gaze to his lips as she raised her hips to rub herself against him.

His eyes fluttered shut, and he gave himself over to the sweet feel of her. "Lord, Ali," he breathed. "Where did you learn to do that?"

She laughed softly. "Some juvenile delinquent taught me a million years ago."

"The kid should be punished." He groaned as she arched a little higher, rubbing a little harder. "Severely punished."

"What did you have in mind?"

He answered with a kiss, shifting sideways to slide a hand to the vee between her thighs. She whimpered, a low, delicious sound of pleasure.

"Turnabout is fair play," he whispered, barely recognizing his own voice.

He worked his fingers against the fabric of her slacks and felt her arch and move against him. Drawing back, just enough to watch her eyes—those beautiful copper eyes of hers that were as dark and tarnished now as old pennies. He brought her to the brink, and stopped.

She groaned, and he lifted his hand to frame her face. "Something wrong?"

"You're a tease."

He laughed softly and shifted to undo the single button of her slacks and slide down the zipper. Beneath was another bit of silk and lace that matched her bra. With a grin, he slid his hand beneath the waistband of her panties. "Darlin', you ain't seen nothin' yet." He touched her with the tips of his fingers, a feather-light touch meant to tantalize.

She gasped and dug her nails into his shoulder. It was almost too much, more than he could take. He hardened to the point of pain as she moved against him and his fingers sank into her slick folds. But watching her, seeing her eyes darken and flutter shut, hearing her soft sounds of ecstasy and feeling the damp heat around his fingers held him back. This time he didn't stop. He teased and toyed until she trembled and groaned and finally exploded in his arms.

He waited while she caught her breath and the tremors that rippled through her body subsided. Finally she opened her eyes, soft now and so beautiful. "Jake?"

He kissed her lightly. "That's just the beginning."

Lowering one foot to the floor, he half stood, half knelt as he slipped his hands beneath the waistband of her slacks and dragged them down and off. He stopped for a moment, thinking how beautiful she was with nothing more than those champagne-colored panties covering her. Then he stripped them off, as well, and shucked his jeans. Pausing only to remove the foil packet from his wallet, he rejoined her on the couch.

"Ali," he said, touching her hair gently, almost reverently. "If you want to change your mind about this…"

She pressed a finger to his lips, then took the packet from his hand. While he watched, she ripped it open and sheathed him in the protective latex with long, slow strokes of her fingers. He hardened further beneath her hand, but she never took her eyes from his. Then she wrapped her arms around his neck and said, "Make love to me, Jake."

He moved over her, wanting to make the moment last as long as possible and to look into her eyes as he made her his. Then he slipped inside her, slow and easy, feeling as if he'd been lost and finally found his way home.

ALI SIGHED AND SETTLED contentedly on Jake's shoulder.

She'd been right. Over the years she'd told herself that making love to Jake couldn't possibly be as she remembered. She'd convinced herself that her memories were skewed by the fact he'd been her first lover and the father of her daughter. Well, now she knew the truth. Making love with Jake wasn't what she remembered. It was better.

She felt like a new woman, warm and wonderful and sexy. And she had Jake to thank for that, for reminding her what it felt like to be wanted by a man.

She'd also found something of herself that she had thought she'd lost. Over the years she'd begun to believe there was something wrong with her because she wasn't interested in sex. Now she knew better. She understood again what it was like to want someone desperately, to need to feel a man inside you. If for no other reason than that, she couldn't regret making love to Jake—even if she never found another man who made her feel this way.

As for the consequences of sleeping with Jake, she felt confident she could deal with them. She wasn't the same starry-eyed girl she'd once been. She didn't need promises for the future. She'd made her own future and was content with it. And as long as she didn't make the same mistake she'd made twelve years ago and get her heart involved, she'd be okay. She could enjoy Jake until one or both of them lost interest, then move on.

"Hey," he said, lifting his free hand to caress her head. "I'm starved."

She laughed softly. "Still?"

Slipping out from under her, he rose up on one arm. "I'm not sure I'll ever get enough of you." He kissed her briefly. "But at the moment, I need food."

"Well," she said with a grin, "I can't do anything about that unless you let me up off this couch."

He ran his gaze down her naked body and grinned. "If I let you up, will you promise to cook like that?"

"Hah." She pushed him off her and grabbed his shirt from the pile of their discarded clothing. "Not on your life." She pulled the shirt on and stood, checking to make sure it covered all the essentials. It hit her mid-thigh.

"What do you think?" she asked.

"It never looked that good on me."

She laughed and headed for the kitchen. She'd

never felt more brazen. And sexy. She was definitely feeling sexy.

Jake pulled on his jeans and followed. "Why don't we skip the steaks," he said, coming up behind her and grabbing her waist as she reached for the refrigerator.

She leaned back against him, and he moved his hands up to cup her breasts through the shirt. "I thought you were starved," she said, laughing.

"I am." He stepped back and moved her away from the refrigerator. "Let me make one of my world-famous omelets. It's quick and easy, and then we can get back to more important matters."

Turning within his grasp, she shifted closer until her thinly covered breast brushed against his bare chest. "What more important matters did you have in mind?"

With a low groan, he drew her back into his arms. "You're a witch."

"Maybe." With her hands on his shoulders, she lifted up to brush her lips against his. "But you like it."

Taking hold of her bare bottom, he pulled her against his arousal. "Oh, yeah." He lowered his mouth to her throat and nipped not too gently. "I like it a lot."

Ali laughed, loving the feel of him. His mouth on her skin, his hands kneading her buttocks and the hard male part of him rubbing against her belly. With a deliciously wicked grin she pushed out of his arms and stepped back. "Okay, back to cooking dinner."

"Forget dinner." He reached for her, but she slid out of reach.

"I'm hungry," she insisted.

He made another grab for her, but she laughed and darted behind the kitchen table, putting three feet of solid oak between them. "Down, boy. We need to eat."

"You really are a witch." He glowered at her and planted his hands on his hips. "Okay, we'll eat. But now you have no choice. It's my omelet or nothing."

Ali crossed her arms, very aware that the movement lifted the shirt to nearly indecent heights. "No fair. You cooked breakfast."

"And you cooked lunch." His gaze followed the direction of the shirt, and she could almost see him calculating what it would take to catch her.

"I made ham sandwiches," she objected, though she knew neither one of them gave a hoot about food at the moment, or who cooked what.

"And I'm going to make you the best omelet you've ever had." He headed for the refrigerator, yanked open the door and started grabbing ingredients. A few seconds later, he turned with arms loaded and closed the door with his knee. "Now, make yourself useful and set the table. Dinner will be ready in ten minutes. Unless you get in my way, then I'm going to take you up on that offer whether you meant it or not."

She laughed and took his warning seriously.

As for the omelet, he hadn't lied. It was delicious and so, she decided, was eating dinner at midnight with a half-naked man. They'd taken the food into the living area, where Jake had built up the fire again, and they'd eaten sitting cross-legged on the floor in front of the coffee table.

Later, they pulled cushions from the couch and lay together on the floor in front of the fire, wrapped in an afghan and each other's arms. They made love again, slowly this time, reacquainting themselves with each other's bodies. Afterward, Ali remained in Jake's arms with her head on his shoulder, happy that at least this once she'd ignored her common sense.

JAKE LAY AWAKE LONG AFTER Ali fell asleep in his arms.

The night before he'd questioned his feelings for her. He'd wondered whether what he felt was leftover love, something new, or merely lust. Now he knew it was all these things. Somehow the past and present had collided, becoming all mixed up in this one woman. Ali.

As a young man, he'd loved her kindness and loyalty, but mostly, he'd needed her light.

He thought about the time before he'd come to Lost Springs, about the dingy little apartment in Cheyenne with its stale smells of liquor, cigarettes and sex. He remembered the woman who had been his mother, old and used-up before her time, and the feel of her fist. And there was the street, where he'd survived any way he could, until the authorities had caught him and sent him to Lost Springs Ranch and Bob Duncan.

Bob Duncan had saved his life, but it had been Ali who'd given him hope. For a boy like him, who'd never experienced her kind of goodness, she'd been a beacon in the night.

And she still was. Only now, she'd become so much more. She'd become a woman rich in strength and confidence, a woman a man could love forever.

And lust?

He couldn't possibly want a woman more. She was a stirring mixture of heat and innocence that aroused both his need to love her and his need to protect her. A compelling combination that had the power to bring him to his knees at her feet and keep him there. He'd told her that he didn't know if he would ever get enough of her. He'd lied. He *knew* he could never get enough.

But was loving her and wanting her enough? For either of them?

He again glanced around her grandfather's cabin. *Her* cabin. He wished he could say that it didn't bother him that he had nothing to give Ali, that he would probably never have anything to give her. But he'd be lying to himself. The concern kept rearing its ugly head, despite his efforts to put it aside.

But could he walk away?

He shifted his head to look at the woman in his arms and felt his body stir to life once again. She was as beautiful and innocent as a child in her sleep.

Not yet.

He couldn't walk away yet. He wanted just a little more time with her, a little more time in the light.

*Fool*, a voice inside him whispered, along with warnings of how he would hurt them both if he didn't forget her. But another part of him, the part he chose to listen to, told him he'd been given a second chance.

And this time, he'd better not blow it.

ALI WOKE SUDDENLY with a sense of foreboding.

She lay for a moment, trying to pinpoint what had awakened her and why she suddenly felt so uneasy. From the cabin came the usual nighttime sounds, the low pop of the dying fire, the mechanical hum of the refrigerator, a mountain breeze brushing against he outside shutters. And there was the soft snore of the man lying beside her. She turned to look at him for a moment and smiled. She'd never slept with a man before, and it was a delicious feeling.

Still, the sense of something wrong overrode even that warmth.

Easing herself out of Jake's arms, she rose and slipped on his shirt again. It smelled of him, and for a moment eased her anxiety. Quietly, she made her way to the front windows.

Dawn wasn't far off. The eastern sky held the first pearly promise of day, and soon the creek would be shimmering with sparks of sunlight and the pines alive with birdsong. The night had been worth all the risk, and she wondered where today would take them. She had a few concerns about how making love would affect their relationship, and how Jake would react once he learned about Samantha. But this odd sensation was something else entirely.

Something she couldn't make sense of.

"What is it, Ali?"

She turned toward Jake, who'd risen up on one arm from their nest on the floor. "No, don't get up," she said, and walked back to rejoin him.

As she sank back to the floor next to him, he reached out and brushed her hair away from her cheek. "Do you regret last night? Is that it?"

For a moment she didn't answer, distracted by this other niggling fear. Then she forced a smile and shook her head. "No." And she realized it was true. Nothing about this weekend had turned out as she planned, but she couldn't regret it, either. She had her answers.

She bent forward and kissed him lightly. "No regrets."

Drawing her closer, he deepened the kiss and started to lower her once again to the floor.

It was time to tell him about Sam. She'd put it off long enough, and maybe this was what was bothering her. Her need to tell him about his daughter. "No, wait, Jake, there's something I have to tell you."

He nipped at her mouth while unbuttoning his shirt. "Did you ask if you could borrow this again?" He pushed aside the fabric, and the cool morning air struck her breasts. "Later," he whispered, and closed his mouth over one puckered nipple. "We'll talk later."

Ali sighed, and the unnamed fear that had dogged her since waking fled before the feel of his mouth on her. "Later," she agreed, and wove her fingers into his hair.

They took their time exploring each other. A gentle touch, a soft sigh, a murmured endearment, and he slipped inside her, filling her with more than his body. She felt the corners of her heart open up to him, stretch and welcome him. And she didn't fight it, any of it. She let him in, body, heart and soul. He took her up slowly, to the brink, and then eased back before she fell over. She moaned his name and held on to him, wondering how she'd ever be able to let him go.

Afterward, they fell asleep again, and Ali forgot the fear that had awakened her earlier. Until the phone rang, sharp and intruding, and she sat bolt upright, her heart pounding in her chest.

No one but Gail knew she was here, and Gail wouldn't call unless there was an emergency.

Jake must have sensed her fear because he released her immediately.

Pulling on his shirt once again, she scrambled for the phone. "Hello," she said, her voice frightened and breathless.

"Ali?" It was Gail, but the moment she said Ali's name she broke into tears.

"Gail, what is it?" Ali demanded. Her own voice had taken on a note of panic and she was vaguely aware of Jake coming up to stand behind her. "Is something wrong with Sam?"

"I..." Gail didn't seem able to speak, and a moment later a male voice replaced her tearful one. "Ali?"

"John," Ali said. "What's wrong?"

"It's the kids, Ali."

"Oh, God." Ali sank back against the counter, her legs no longer able to hold her, but suddenly a pair of strong arms was there to support her. "Tell me Sam's okay, John."

"They're missing, Ali."

# CHAPTER SEVEN

JAKE WATCHED ALI'S FACE go chalk-white.

"What do you mean they're missing?" she said into the phone.

Whoever was on the other end of the line spoke in hurried tones. Though Jake couldn't make out the words, he recognized the urgency in the voice. He'd heard it too many times himself to be mistaken.

Suddenly Ali sank against the counter and Jake grabbed her, wrapping his arms around her shoulders to steady her. She began to tremble beneath his hands, and every protective instinct he possessed surfaced. Whatever was wrong, he would fix it for her.

She closed her eyes, visibly making an attempt to get herself under control. "Okay. Yes." She nodded. "Right away. I'm about two hours away. Okay." She turned and grabbed a pencil from the counter and scribbled a number on the back of an envelope.

The disembodied voice on the other end spoke again, and Ali continued to nod as if the movement would somehow keep her from falling apart. "I've got it," she said. "I'll be there as soon as I can." She hung up the phone but stood with her hand on the receiver for several long moments, seemingly unaware of Jake's presence.

"Ali?"

She looked up, but he didn't think she saw him.

Fear filled her eyes along with a well of unshed tears. He couldn't stand seeing her like this and quickly drew her into his arms. She came stiffly at first, then collapsed against him, her tears silently breaking free against his bare chest. He tried to soothe her with nonsensical words, but a feeling of helplessness stole over him as she continued to cry. It wasn't a feeling he was familiar with, but then again, Ali had never wept in his arms before.

"My God, Ali," he begged. "Tell me what's wrong."

"It's Sam." Her voice sounded choked and unsteady.

Sam? Jealousy nipped at his consciousness as a dozen possibilities occurred to him. With an effort, he pushed the unwanted emotion aside. "Who's Sam?"

She stepped back from his embrace, though he didn't think it was a good idea. She was still shaking, and he wasn't sure she could stand on her own. But she made an obvious effort to pull herself together, wiping her eyes with the back of her hand and lifting her chin to look at him. "Sam is short for Samantha. She's my daughter."

The statement hit him square in the chest. Her daughter?

Before he had time to react, Ali was talking again, too fast for him to follow. "Whoa, honey," he said, and grasped her shoulders. "Slow down and start over. Now, tell me what happened."

She choked back a sob, and he reached out to pull her back in his arms. But she held up her hands, palms out. "No, I'm okay."

Jake backed off. "Then tell me."

Ali pressed a hand against her mouth and nodded. Speaking slowly now, she said, "Sam was on a camping trip with a group from her school." She dropped her hand from her face and crossed her arms over her chest, as if trying to physically hold herself together. "This morning when Gail went in to wake the girls in Sam's tent..." She hesitated, pressed her lips together briefly and pushed on. "Sam was gone."

Again, Ali took a moment to get herself under control, all except the trembling, which she seemed unable to stop. "Then Gail checked her son Paul's tent, and he was gone, too. Along with another boy named Brad Gibbons." Ali caught her bottom lip between her teeth, then released it. "Gail knew if Sam had taken off, so had Paul."

"How did she know that?"

"They're best friends and pretty much inseparable." A faint smile broke through her tears. "One wouldn't go without the other."

"Did they start a search?" he asked.

"Gail said they looked for two hours before calling the authorities."

Jake backed up a bit and ran a hand through his hair. He had another question he hated asking, but he needed to know what they were up against. "Any signs of foul play?"

She shook her head. "Gail said the kids rigged their sleeping bags to look like they were in them. She thinks they took off sometime during the night."

Jake took a deep, relieved breath. At least they weren't dealing with some maniac, only kids pulling a foolish stunt, which was a small comfort. Either way, the outcome could end up the same—though he refused to consider that possibility. Not yet, anyway.

But he needed more information. "Were there other kids in the tents?"

"I think so."

"And they don't know anything?"

Again she shook her head, and fresh tears ran down her face. "That's all I know, Jake. I have to get over there."

"I'm sorry. Of course you do." He pulled her back into his arms. "And don't worry, we'll find them. I promise." For a few moments more he held her, his mind racing. They had very little time to waste. The longer those kids were in the mountains alone, the less chance anyone had of finding them alive. "Now," he said, when Ali seemed to have herself under control again, "I want you to go upstairs and get dressed. We need to get going."

"You don't—"

He squeezed her shoulders to silence her protest. "This isn't the time to be stubborn, Ali. Not only are you in no condition to drive, you need me." He gently pushed her toward the stairs. "Go on now and get ready."

As she headed for her room, it struck him again— Ali had a daughter.

A dozen questions popped into his mind. Hell, more than a dozen, but one loomed larger than all the rest. Who was the father? Yesterday Ali had told him she'd had no serious relationships in the last twelve years, but there must have been at least one. One serious enough to give her a child. Again a flood of jealousy almost got the best of him, but he nipped it in the bud. He had no right to be jealous of Ali. He'd given her up a long time ago.

But why would she lie to him?

That question pecked at him until another thought pushed to the surface. Now wasn't the time. He needed to put his curiosity about Ali and her daughter aside and concentrate on finding those three missing children. Later, after they found the kids, there would be plenty of time to ask Ali for an explanation. Meanwhile, he needed answers to a whole different set of questions.

Taking the number she'd written down on the envelope, he picked up the phone.

IT HAD ONLY BEEN thirty minutes since Ali had gotten the call that spun the day on its axis, but it felt like thirty hours. And Jake knew from experience that before the sun set, it would feel like thirty more.

As they climbed into his Jeep, he glanced at the sky. It was clear and blue, but he sensed a heaviness in the air that made him uneasy. He hadn't taken time to check the weather, but maybe he should have. The one thing that could make this situation worse was a storm. But there was no point in mentioning that now. It would only give Ali more to worry about, and he could be wrong.

Dear God, let him be wrong.

They took the road heading north to Douglas where they'd catch Highway 94 going back down the east side of the Laramie Mountains. The camp was just outside the town of Esterbrook. Ali seemed to be operating on autopilot, and again Jake felt at a loss as to how to deal with her. Which was foolish. He dealt with distraught relatives all the time. This was no different.

Except this time, it was Ali.

He glanced over at her. She sat rigidly next to the

passenger door, staring out the side window. Somehow between the time he'd sent her upstairs to get dressed and when she'd returned ready to leave, she'd taken strict charge of her emotions. She'd even managed to dress in sensible layers for what might end up being a long vigil. But he had only to look at her pale face with its red-rimmed eyes, or her hands clasped tightly in her lap, to know how hard she struggled to maintain that control.

"Can we go faster?" she asked, evidently sensing him looking at her.

Jake turned his attention back to his driving. "Not until we reach the highway." They had fifteen miles of gravel road to cover before they hit pavement, and unless they wanted to end up in a ditch, he needed to keep the four-wheel drive at a reasonable speed.

She didn't argue—although he almost wished she would. Instead she continued her blank perusal of the landscape. The silence wasn't good for either of them. It gave him too much time to worry about questions that were unimportant now, and it gave her too much time to imagine all the possible ways a child could get hurt in the mountains.

"Ali," he said, "tell me about this camping trip."

For a moment he didn't think she'd answer. Then she sighed. "The Lander Elementary PTA sponsors this trip every year for the seventh and eighth graders."

"So the kids are what? Ten? Eleven?"

She threw him a quick glance but then hastily turned away again. "Some of them. They range from eleven to fourteen."

"Does the whole class go?"

She shook her head. "No, it's a reward. The kids

have to maintain a B average and have less than five disciplinary actions throughout the school year.''

''Disciplinary actions?''

''You know, being written up for bad behavior or being late for class.'' She shrugged. ''That sort of thing.''

Yeah, he remembered. He'd been the king of disciplinary actions when he was in school. Only that hadn't been quite what they'd called being sent to the principal's office back then. ''You must be proud of her. I mean, being good at school and all.''

''Yeah, I am. Sam's pretty much a straight-A student, but the disciplinary actions...'' Ali let out a short, humorless laugh. ''Let's just say it was touch-and-go there for a while as far as her being included on this trip.''

That surprised him. He would have expected Ali's daughter to be the perfect student in every way. Like her mother. ''Does she get into trouble a lot?''

''Well, I wouldn't say a lot. She just tends to be very...social.'' Ali rested her elbow on the window and leaned her head against her hand. ''And she hasn't figured out she's a girl and not supposed to get into fights with boys.''

''She fights with the boys?''

''Only the ones who give her—or someone she likes—a hard time.''

He glanced at Ali and grinned. ''Really?''

''Really.'' *She* didn't seem amused. ''And she usually wins, too.''

He chuckled softly and threw her another glance. ''You got yourself a tomboy.''

A ghost of a smile touched her lips. ''That's one way of putting it.''

"Who'd have guessed?" He laughed again. Would Ali never cease to surprise him? She might have loved the woods and hiking, but she'd been all girl. There had never been any hint of the tomboy in her—at least, not that Jake had seen. Of course, Ali had been sixteen when he first met her, and her daughter was only...

He realized suddenly that he didn't know Sam's age.

He was about to ask when something stopped him, a suspicion he immediately dismissed. Instead, he said, "But Sam did manage to go on the camping trip?"

"Yeah, she squeaked by and was really excited about it."

"What about her friend, Gail's son?"

"Paul? He and Sam are two of a kind. Full of life and into everything." She dropped her hand to her lap and seemed to be thinking about something for a minute. "They've done some crazy things before, but this..." She shook her head. "They both know better. They know how dangerous the mountains are. Especially at night."

"I take it this isn't their first camping trip?"

"No, John...that's Gail's husband, has been taking Paul and his younger brother for years. And since we moved here, he's included Sam. John's spent his whole life in this area and is a real stickler for safety."

Jake thought about that for a while, wondering about kids doing things they knew would get them into trouble or hurt. He'd been that kind of kid, and yet sometimes their thinking baffled even him. He'd decided after years of searching for missing kids that there were as many reasons for risky behavior as there were kids to pull it off. And if he could figure out what made these particular kids tick, maybe he could find them.

"What about the second boy?" he asked. "What was his name? Brad?"

"Yes, Brad Gibbons." She shook her head. "I don't know anything about him. Actually, I've never even heard of him before."

"Isn't that unusual? I mean, the school can't be very big."

"It's not," she agreed. "And it *is* a little unusual that I've never heard Brad's name before. I thought I knew all of Sam's classmates." She shrugged. "Maybe he's just moved to Lightning Creek or something."

Jake glanced at her. "Then why would he be included on this trip?"

"I don't know." She hesitated. "There's something else that bothers me, too. Most of the time Sam and Paul don't include anyone else in their schemes. It's usually just the two of them getting into stuff."

"Unless..."

She looked at him and frowned. "What are you thinking?"

"Well..." He was guessing now, but until he could talk to the other kids on the trip, that's all he could do. "I was just trying to remember what it was like to be that age. Seems to me that kids, especially boys, tend to do things they know they shouldn't on a dare."

She turned back to stare out the window again. "And they can be pretty tough on the new kid."

"Yeah." He took a deep breath and nodded. "That's what I was thinking."

They were coming up on Douglas and the highway that would take them back south on the east side of the mountains. For several minutes as Jake negotiated the transfer from one road to another, they didn't speak. Once they were on a straight road again, he looked back over at Ali and realized she was again struggling to contain her fear.

Reaching across the seat, he took her icy hand in his. "We'll find them, Ali."

She looked at him with frightened eyes. "I should have been there."

"How would that have changed anything? Would Sam have behaved differently if you'd been along?"

"I don't know. Maybe." Ali shook her head and turned back to stare at the passing landscape. He squeezed her hand to get her attention. "Ali?" When she didn't respond, he said, "This is what I do. I find people who are lost."

She bit her lip, and a tear slipped down her cheek. "And sometimes you don't."

He couldn't lie to her. "You're right, sometimes I don't. But I'm very good at what I do." He said it matter-of-factly, trying to reassure her that he'd find her daughter. "And I *will* find Samantha."

Ali wanted to believe him.

She wanted to feel certain that if everyone else failed, Jake would find her daughter. *Their* daughter. Oh, God, why hadn't she told him when she'd had the chance? Now it was too late. Telling him now would be a distraction when he needed clarity most. It wouldn't help any of them if his thoughts were clouded by emotion—either fear of losing the daughter he'd never met, or anger at Ali for keeping that daughter from him. Besides, he was going to find out very soon, anyway.

The moment he saw her.

THE DRIVE SOUTH, from Douglas to Esterbrook Campground, seemed like the longest hour of Ali's life. For a while as she'd talked to Jake, she'd been able to push aside her fear and relegate it to the back of her consciousness. She answered his questions, explaining about the camping trip and telling him about Sam and Paul. She understood he was trying to keep her mind occupied while gathering information that might help him find the missing children, and she was grateful.

Then the silence had descended again, and on its heels the mind-numbing terror.

She fought it with all her strength. Her daughter needed her, and Ali couldn't afford to fall apart now.

Finally Jake turned into the campground, and Ali's pulse began to race. A half-dozen patrol cars and forest service vehicles were scattered around, with all the accompanying personnel. There also seemed to be quite a few people with no official purpose, campers, parents, volunteers or just gawkers. And then there was the news van, professional voyeurs out to record the suffering of others.

Jake wound the Jeep carefully through the crowd and parked near the camp office. Suddenly Ali didn't want to get out of the vehicle.

What if they'd found the kids, and they were hurt or... No, she wouldn't let herself think like that. Besides, if they'd found the children, Gail would have let Ali know. Jake had called John back earlier, spoken to someone on the rescue team and given them his mobile phone number. Ali would know if Sam had been found. But the possibility teased at her thoughts, anyway. What if the rescue team hadn't wanted to break bad news over the phone? As long as Ali stayed within the confines of the truck, she wouldn't have to hear it and face the unthinkable. She could still hope....

Her door opened, and she turned to see Jake holding it.

"Come on, Ali," he said. "Let's go find your daughter and her friends."

For a moment she sat staring at this large man whom she barely knew. She'd once loved him, and last night she'd slept with him, but she had the feeling she was seeing him now for the first time. There was something about him, something solid and calm that made her want to hold on to him, trust him. Like the mountain behind him, he possessed an inner strength that she desperately needed. But by leaning on him, she feared she'd lose a piece of herself.

"Ali," he said again, and she heard the concern and the urgency in his voice.

Feeling foolish, she climbed out of the vehicle. When had she turned into such a basket case? She'd always prided herself on her strength. Now she was acting like a total ninny. Then again, some malicious part of her consciousness reminded her, she'd never had to face the possibility of losing Sam before.

"You okay?" Jake asked.

She nodded and gave him a tight smile. "I'll be fine."

"Ali!"

They both turned toward the female voice. It was

Gail, red-eyed and frantic looking as she closed the distance between them. "Oh, Ali, you're finally here."

"We got here as quickly as we could." Ali wrapped her arms around her distraught friend as she gave in to the tears. "It's okay," Ali said with more assurance than she felt. "We'll find them."

Pulling back, but still keeping hold of Gail's shoulders, she added, "Look at all these people here, all these experts. And—" she motioned toward the man at her side "—I brought Jake. He's one of the best. He's going to find Sam and Paul." Somehow the act of comforting Gail helped Ali, as well. It gave her a measure of control over her emotions that she hadn't experienced since getting the phone call this morning. Gail needed her, and Ali wouldn't let the other woman down.

"I'm so sorry, Ali," Gail said, glancing at Jake and back again. "This is all my fault."

"Don't be ridiculous, Gail." Ali gave her friend's shoulders one final squeeze before releasing her. "How could you have known that Sam and Paul would pull something like this?"

Gail shook her head. "I should have done something."

"That's crazy," Ali said. "Now, what about John? Where is he?"

Gail retrieved a crumpled tissue from her pocket and dabbed at her eyes. "He went out with one of the teams right after we called you."

"That's good," Jake said. "He's more likely to know where the kids would have gone than anyone else."

Gail nodded, making an effort to pull herself together. "Funny, I was fine until you showed up. Now I'm like a leaking faucet."

Ali smiled, understanding completely. She, too, was most likely to lose control when someone close offered sympathy. Knowing that, she changed the subject and said, "Tell us what else is going on."

Gail glanced at Jake, then turned back to Ali. "When I found the kids gone this morning, we started looking right away. But at first..." She shook her head. "I was more angry than worried. John has brought the kids here a lot, and they know the area fairly well. I figured they'd gone off somewhere without permission and would be back by the time we got breakfast started." She looked at Ali with pleading eyes. "You know how Sam and Paul are."

Ali nodded and slipped an arm around Gail's shoulders. "Yes, I know."

"Anyway," Gail continued, "two hours later, I called the authorities." She nodded toward the building behind them. "They're coordinating the search from the office. There have been volunteers coming in all morning." Again, she looked at Jake. "They can tell you more about what's being done."

"What about the other kids in the tent?" Jake asked. "Has anyone talked to them?"

Gail let out a short, humorless laugh. "Everyone. The tents sleep four, so there were three other girls in Sam's tent and two boys in with Paul and Brad. None of them seem to know anything."

"What about Brad?" Ali asked. "Is he new in school?"

"No," Gail answered. "He's staying here for the summer with his aunt."

"Then why was he on the trip?" Jake asked.

"Technically, he shouldn't have been," Gail admitted. "But evidently his father is a wealthy businessman from Seattle, and he approached the PTA board last week and offered to pay for the entire weekend if we agreed to take Brad with us."

Ali wondered why she hadn't heard anything about this. "And the board agreed?"

Gail shrugged. "We're a small town with limited resources. Yeah, it seemed like a good deal to us."

"Did the other kids resent him being here?" Jake asked.

Gail thought about that for a moment before answering. "Maybe a bit at first, but they seemed to accept him after a while."

"What about his aunt?" Ali asked. "Is she here?"

"We haven't been able to reach her."

That seemed strange to Ali. If the woman was responsible for her nephew for the summer, wouldn't she make sure she could be reached in case of an emergency? "What about his parents?"

"His mother's deceased, but we have a call in to his father."

"Are the other kids from Sam and Paul's tent still here?" Jake asked.

"A few," Gail answered. "But most of the parents have already arrived and taken them home."

Jake frowned and ran a hand through his hair. "Can you make sure those that are still here stay a bit longer? I need to go find out what the search team is doing, but I really want to talk to those kids, as well."

"Sure," Gail agreed.

"Will you be okay for a few minutes if I go with Jake?" Ali asked.

"I'll be fine." Motioning toward a picnic table where a group of adults and kids had gathered, she added, "I'll be over there."

Ali gave her friend another quick hug before following Jake into the camp office. It looked like a command center straight out of a war movie, with radio equipment and a large map of the immediate area tacked up on the wall. Multicolored pins had been stuck into the map, and a man stood instructing a group of three volunteers.

Jake waited until they'd finished before approaching the man, who was obviously in charge. "I'm Jake Merrill," he said, holding out his hand. "We talked on the phone a couple of hours ago."

"Tom Bowman." The man grasped Jake's hand then suddenly smiled. "I know you. I thought your name sounded familiar when we talked. You're the guy who pulled that family out of their truck last spring. The one that got caught in the flash flood. It was all over the news."

Jake crammed his hands into the back pockets of his jeans and threw Ali an uneasy glance. "I was just doing my job. Like you're doing here."

"But..." Bowman protested, then looked apologetically at Ali, obviously realizing this wasn't the time or place. "Sorry, ma'am."

"It's okay," she answered, actually pleased with the bit of trivia about Jake. Under different circumstances, she'd want to know more.

Taking her arm, Jake drew her alongside him. "This is Alison Kendrick. Her daughter Samantha is one of the missing children."

"Nice to meet you, Ms. Kendrick. I want you to

know we're doing everything we can to find those kids.''

"I know you are.''

"Can you tell me what you have here?'' Jake motioned toward the map on the wall. "And what I can do to help?''

"Sure can,'' Bowman said. "And we can use all the help we can get. Especially the experienced kind.'' He became all business as he explained the strategy for finding the three missing children. Jake listened carefully, asking questions Ali would never have thought of and making suggestions the other man considered and often agreed with.

After a few minutes, Jake asked, "How long before the helicopter arrives?''

Bowman glanced at his watch. "Twenty, twenty-five minutes, maybe.''

"I'd like to go up,'' Jake said. "I'm not familiar with these mountains, so I wouldn't be much use on the ground.''

"Well, I don't know about that,'' Bowman countered. "But you're welcome to go up in the chopper, anyway. I've only got one man trained for aerial search, and he hasn't checked in yet. But the pilot knows the area.''

"Good. Meanwhile,'' Jake said, "I want to talk to the other campers. Especially the ones sharing the kids' tents.''

"Sure.'' Bowman shrugged. "We've already talked to them, but feel free. You've got time before the chopper gets here.''

"Thanks, I'll be ready.'' Taking Ali's arm again, Jake led her outside.

As they stepped out of the small wooden building,

a low roll of thunder sounded in the distance. Ali glanced at the western horizon and felt a chill despite the warmth of the day. This time of year, late-afternoon thunderstorms were a common occurrence in the mountains.

"Jake." She put all her reawakened fear into his name.

"Come on," he said without taking his eyes off the distant clouds. "We don't have any time to lose."

They hurried over to where Gail sat on a picnic table amid a half-dozen kids and several other adults. She seemed to have herself under control now and gave them a tight smile. "Any news?"

Ali shook her head. "Not yet. Jake wants to talk to the girls sharing Sam's tent," she explained. "And the two boys with Brad and Paul."

"I was in Sam's tent," a small blond girl piped up. "But Beth and Darlene have already gone home."

"And the boys, too," Gail added. "Their parents came and got them."

Ali saw frustration flicker across Jake's features, but she tried not to let it bother her. After all, Gail had said everyone else had already talked to the kids. Still, Jake might have learned something useful.

Hiding her disappointment, Ali smiled at the girl. "Jake, this is Rachel Byers. She's a year ahead of Sam in school. Rachel, this is Mr. Merrill."

"Do you mind answering a few questions, Rachel?" Jake asked.

"I already told Mrs. Sebring and the other guy everything I know," she answered. "Which isn't much."

Jake sat down on the bench next to the girl. "Well, maybe you know more than you think."

"Like in the movies?"

Jake nodded. "Yeah, something like that. Now, tell me how Sam was acting last night."

"Like she always acts."

"Well, you see, Rachel—" Jake rubbed his chin "—I've never met Samantha. So I don't know how she usually acts. How about if you fill me in."

"She was complaining about Brad Gibbons." Rachel shook her head and gave him a wide-eyed stare. "She was always complaining about one of the boys."

"Really?" That seemed to catch Jake's attention.

"I thought he was kind of cute," Rachel confessed. "But she said he was stuck-up."

"He kept bragging about how much money his dad has," added one of the boys.

Jake looked at the boy, frowned and turned back to Rachel. "So, if Sam and Brad weren't getting along, why did they all go off together?"

Ali was asking herself the same question.

"Oh, I didn't say they weren't getting along," Rachel said. "They were real chummy yesterday afternoon. All three of them. Her, Paul and Brad."

It didn't make any sense, Ali thought. Either Sam and Paul were getting along with Brad or they weren't.

"There was one other thing I thought was strange," Rachel said, glancing at Ali and looking a little embarrassed. "I told the other man but he didn't think much of it."

"What was that?" Jake asked.

"Sam went to sleep last night before any of the rest of us. She never does that."

Jake glanced at Ali for confirmation, and she nodded. "She fights sleep."

"Did you think she was sick?" he asked, turning back to Rachel.

Rachel shrugged. "She didn't act sick."

"We figured that was their way of setting everyone up," Gail said. "They pretended to go to sleep, then when the other kids settled down, they rigged their sleeping bags and took off."

"That makes sense," Jake agreed. "What about..." But the sound of an approaching helicopter cut him off.

Ali followed his gaze to the aircraft as it slowly settled down in an open field. Again she noticed the dark clouds, and a fresh wave of fear threatened to overwhelm her. In the few minutes while she and Jake had been talking to the kids, it seemed the storm had come miles closer.

"Well, I've got to go," Jake said, giving Rachel a big smile. "Thanks for the help."

The girl beamed, and Ali went with Jake as he started across the camp toward the waiting helicopter. Once they were out of earshot of the others, Ali took hold of his arm. "Jake, I'm coming with you."

He kept walking. "You need to stay here."

"I can't stay here," she insisted. "I need to do something."

Finally he stopped and turned to face her. "You need to be here in case one of the other teams finds Sam." She planted her hands on her hips, but before she could say anything, he added, "Besides..." He reached up and brushed her cheek. "If you come, you'll be in my way."

She started to object, but he cut her off. "Stay here,

Ali. This is where you're needed. I'll find your daughter."

How many times in the last few hours had he said those exact words to her? What would he say or do if he knew Sam was his daughter, as well? Would it make him search harder? No, one thing she believed; Jake would do his best to find the children, no matter what. The danger lay in telling him about Sam and possibly distracting him.

As for going with him, she considered arguing further but realized he was right. If some other team brought Sam in, Ali needed to be here for her daughter. "Okay." She nodded and backed away. "You'll call as soon as you know something."

He leaned down and kissed her. "You bet."

A bit stunned, Ali backed up as he climbed into the helicopter. Even with all that was going on, he had the power to render her speechless with nothing more than a brief kiss.

Gail stepped up beside her as the helicopter lifted off the ground. "You two got along fairly well, I see."

Ali felt her cheeks heat. She'd been so preoccupied with Jake that she hadn't heard the other woman approach. "Yes."

"He doesn't know Sam's his daughter, does he?"

Something tightened in Ali's chest. "I never got around to telling him. Then when you called..."

Gail let the silence settle for a few moments before saying, "It's probably better that he doesn't know. It'll keep him focused."

"I hope so."

"You know he'll figure it out the minute he sees her."

Ali nodded. Right now, she couldn't think of anything she wanted more.

# CHAPTER EIGHT

THE STORM WAS COMING IN FAST.

Jake watched the dark clouds roll steadily over the mountains, obliterating the sky inch by inch. If they didn't find those kids soon, the chances of finding them at all were pretty slim. Not only would the storm make continuing the search impossible, the wind and rain would erase any signs of them. And unless they'd found some kind of shelter, Jake doubted whether they could survive another night in the mountains.

"Where to now?" the pilot called over the noise of the rotors.

They'd been up for almost two hours and would soon have to return to base to refuel, but Jake refused to give up. Ali and those kids were depending on him, and he wasn't going to let them down.

"Let's check out those bluffs below the camp again," Jake said. "They're close enough to the campground that the kids could have easily reached them, and there are a lot of places where they could be hidden among those rocks."

"We've been over that area a half-dozen times already," the pilot countered.

"Let's try and get closer this time."

Thunder rumbled overhead and a flash of lightning touched the horizon. A gust of wind toyed with the helicopter, and the pilot struggled for a few seconds to steady it. "If this keeps up," he called to Jake, "we could end up in a ditch ourselves."

Jake met the pilot's gaze and held it. "If we don't find those kids soon, there's very little question how *they'll* end up."

The other man took a deep breath, nodded and swung the chopper back around. Obviously he, too, understood how little time they had left.

As they came up on the area, Jake scanned the ground at the bottom of the rugged rock wall. Nothing. Just as before. But something kept drawing him back here. Call it gut instinct or whatever, he'd learned over the years not to ignore it. Besides, they could fly over this area all day and still not spot the kids—if they happened to be in the wrong place. The landscape was riddled with granite boulders and deep vertical fissures, any one of which could hide an injured child. Or three.

With a thumbs-up, he motioned for the pilot to fly higher along the precipice. The helicopter started to rise, keeping as close as possible to the cliff face.

Movement.

"There." Jake's heart thudded wildly as he pointed toward a particularly rough section of rock about a quarter of the way down the granite bluff. "I think I saw something. Can you steady this bird and bring us a bit closer?"

The pilot worked the controls, and Jake trained his binoculars on the spot where he thought he'd seen a brief flash of color. For several seconds he didn't see anything else and was beginning to think he'd been hallucinating, hoping to see life where there was none. Then he saw it again, at the bottom of a crevice.

"I think we found them." Relief washed over him

as he moved the binoculars over the area. Then a sick feeling settled in the pit of his stomach. "Damn."

IT HAD BEEN TWO HOURS since Jake had taken off in the helicopter. Two hours of misery. Two hours without a word.

Along with Gail and the few remaining campers, Ali had taken refuge from the approaching storm inside the office. She'd been pacing for some time, a cup of lukewarm coffee in her hand, feeling powerless. The waiting was killing her.

She wanted to do something.

"Esterbrook, do you read me? Esterbrook?" Jake's voice crackled over the radio.

For a breathless moment, everyone in the room froze. Then Bowman grabbed the microphone, and the rest of them crowded around. "Esterbrook here. We read you, Jake. Go ahead."

"We found..." Static broke up the reception, but it couldn't still the rush of hope brought by his words. Or the fear.

"Come again, Jake," Bowman said. "You're breaking up."

More static crackled on the line. "The storm..." As if to emphasize his words, a crack of thunder shook the office.

Dread settled in Ali's stomach right next to the hope.

"Come again, Jake," Bowman repeated.

No one in the room dared breathe as the line continued to pop and crackle. Then Jake's voice came across clear and loud. "We found them."

Palpable relief washed through the group, but they

stifled their cries of joy, trying to hear the rest of Jake's message.

"We've got two in good shape, and—" again static interfered "—one down."

AT THE BOTTOM of the crevice, two small figures stood waving at the helicopter. Behind them, the third child lay beneath a nearby ledge, unmoving. Jake tried to remain unemotional while silently praying the one on the ground wasn't Ali's daughter. Then he felt instantly contrite. He couldn't wish for any of these kids to be seriously hurt.

"Is the one on the ground alive?" asked the pilot.

"Can't tell." Jake raised his binoculars to the wall of rock above the kids and cursed.

"How the hell did they get down there?" the pilot asked.

Jake studied the area above the kids, who continued to frantically wave at them. "Looks like they slid. Got a rock slide and what looks like very unstable ground above them." He focused again on the narrow fissure and wondered how many times they'd flown over and not spotted the children. He'd been lucky to catch sight of them this time. The crevice was deep and narrow, not much more than a slender crack in the granite, with outcrops of rock that hid most of the bottom from above.

"There's no way I can set down there," the pilot said unnecessarily.

Jake had been on enough helicopter rescue operations to have a fair idea of what a pilot could and couldn't do with his aircraft. This pilot was good, but that didn't mean a thing if the ground was too rugged or there wasn't room to clear the rotors. One way or another, Jake was going to have to climb. "What about up top?" he asked.

The pilot brought the helicopter up the cliff face, hovered a minute or two, then shook his head. "There's not enough room, and what's there looks pretty unstable. We could end up bringing the whole thing down on their heads if I even try."

Jake cursed silently and studied the area around the kids. "I need to get them."

"If you try and climb down, it could have the same results as trying to land," the pilot countered. "You could end up stuck at the bottom with them, or burying them under another rock slide."

Jake knew the other man was right and could see only one other way to get those kids out of that hole. "We're going to have to climb *up* to them."

The pilot shook his head. "Not until the storm passes, you're not."

Jake weighed his options. He knew the pilot was right. Climbing up that cliff in the middle of a storm would be extremely dangerous. And forget bringing the kids down. They'd have to be carried, one on a stretcher. Even the best climber could lose his footing on slippery rock and end up falling. But Jake couldn't leave them there alone, either.

"Okay, I tell you what," Jake said. "I'm going down on the winch." He pointed to a relatively flat area a few degrees to the right of the crevice where the kids had fallen. "Over there."

The pilot shot him a guarded glance but seemed willing to listen.

"I'll take food, blankets and medical supplies," Jake said. "Whatever I can carry on my back."

"That won't be much."

"It'll have to do. I'll climb across to the kids and do what I can for them. Meanwhile, you go and get a team together, and be back here as soon as the storm passes."

"Are you sure?" the pilot asked.

Jake took a deep breath. "I don't have any other choice."

The other man hesitated, then nodded, obviously resigned that there was no way of changing Jake's mind.

Meanwhile, Jake began loading as much as he could into a large pack. He put in three lightweight thermal blankets, an emergency medical kit, packages of dried soup and instant hot chocolate, a few utensils, and a small, portable kerosene cook stove. When he was done, he signaled the pilot to move the aircraft into position.

Even under the best of conditions Jake wasn't fond of climbing into a harness and trusting a cable to lower him safely from a hovering helicopter. He knew there were guys who got off on it, the thrill of flirting with danger, but he wasn't one of them. And on a day like today, with the storm moving in and buffeting the chopper with gusts of wind, it was pretty damn scary. The pilot had gotten as close to the ground as possible, but that wasn't nearly close enough. The cable swayed wildly as Jake started his descent, ever-conscious of the rock wall, which, if hit, could end this little escapade before it even got started.

He kept his mind on the kids and the need to reach them. If the approaching storm was working its terror on him, he could only imagine what it was doing to those three children alone on the side of the mountain.

When his feet finally touched solid ground, he said a little prayer of thanks and quickly unhooked the harness. Then, giving the pilot a thumbs-up, he watched as the chopper pulled up and headed back to camp.

Now that he was down, he could see that under normal circumstances the climb into the crevice would be fairly easy. Unfortunately, these weren't normal circumstances. Again the weather was working against him. That and the rock slide that had left the ridge above the kids unstable. But Jake didn't have time to worry too much about either problem. As fast as he dared, he went in from the side where the ground seemed to be more solid, hoping to reach the bottom before the storm broke.

He was almost down when the skies opened up, sending rivers of icy water into the narrow fissure. He half slid, half fell the last twenty feet or so and crossed the narrow rock floor at a full run. From under the protection of a ledge, two sets of hopeful eyes watched him come.

"Are you all right?" he asked as he made a quick assessment of the two children. The girl, Ali's daughter, had a few cuts and bruises but otherwise seemed unscathed. The boy, on the other hand, favored his ankle.

"We're okay," Samantha answered anxiously. "But Brad's hurt."

Jake moved to the boy on the ground, who lay near the cliff face under the overhang. "Has he been unconscious the whole time?"

"He wakes up every now and then," Paul said. "That's how we got him under the ledge."

"It was cold, and we were trying to keep him warm," Sam explained.

Jake nodded and quickly examined Brad, checking for broken bones or indications of internal bleeding. He found neither. However, there was a bump on his head that hinted at why he remained unconscious. But what the boy needed was a doctor. All Jake could do was try to keep him warm until help arrived.

Pulling the blankets from his pack, he handed a couple to Sam and Paul and tucked the third around Brad. As he was finishing up, Brad stirred and opened his eyes.

"Can you hear me?" Jake asked.

Brad nodded.

"Where does it hurt?"

"My head. And I'm so...tired." Brad's eyelids fluttered closed.

"Come on, Brad," Jake urged. "Try and stay awake."

"I want my dad." With that, he slipped off to sleep.

Failing to reawaken him, Jake turned to the other two children to see what he could do to make them more comfortable. They'd wrapped themselves in the blankets and were huddled together as far beneath the ledge as possible. The storm was in full force now, and he needed to make sure they stayed dry and as warm as possible. He managed to get the cook stove lit and heated the packages of soup and chocolate to get something hot and nourishing into their systems. Then he looked at Paul's ankle, which was swollen and discolored, and bound it with an Ace bandage.

After that, there was nothing to do but wait.

As for Samantha, he should have recognized her

immediately, and under different circumstances he might have. Instead, he'd been so busy getting them settled that it didn't strike him until later.

They were sitting around their minuscule fire while Sam and Paul related how they'd come to the bottom of this rocky crevice. Sam lifted those wide dark eyes to Jake, telling him about the mountain lion they'd encountered, and he saw remembered fear as well as excitement in her expression. And he knew. As clearly and surely as if he'd been there at her birth.

Samantha was *his* daughter.

FOR ALI, THE DAY SEEMED to stretch on forever.

She and Gail had sat side by side in the small office cabin, holding on to each other's hands as if their lives—and their children's—depended on it. First they'd waited for word from any one of the half-dozen ground teams, or from Jake leading the aerial search. When Jake's static-filled voice had come over the radio, they'd hoped for something more. One of the three children had been injured, but which child or how badly hurt, no one knew.

The helicopter had returned a short time later in the midst of the first onslaught of the storm, but the pilot was alone. He'd explained Jake's plan, and while Tom Bowman spent the next hour in activity, preparing a team to climb up and carry the children out, Ali and Gail continued their silent vigil.

It was the worst kind of torment. Waiting. Doing nothing. Not knowing.

Finally, the storm had started to let up and the team set out. Again, there was nothing Ali or Gail could do to help. By now, John had returned, and Gail had fallen into her husband's arms, leaving Ali feeling bereft of her friend's support—and hating herself for feeling that way.

The call finally came hours later.

The climbing team had reached the children. They would be carried down the mountain and airlifted to the hospital in Douglas.

All three were alive and well.

JAKE WAITED AS the paramedics loaded the stretcher with Brad Gibbons's small, unconscious form onto the helicopter. Then Jake climbed into the last remaining seat, slammed the door and gave the pilot a thumbs-up. As the aircraft lifted off the ground, Jake wrapped his arm around the small figure sitting next to him. She settled against his side and fell asleep almost instantly.

Exhaustion tugged at him as well.

His plan had worked. All three children were safe.

They'd fared well under the circumstances—even before he'd gotten to them. All three had warm jackets and they'd known enough to keep out of the wind. It was Brad who had worried Jake as they waited for the storm to abate and the rescue team to reach them. The boy had continued to sleep, waking occasionally for brief periods before falling back into a restless slumber. But once the paramedics had arrived and examined Brad, they'd assured Jake the boy was suffering from a mild concussion and would be fine.

Now the helicopter headed toward Douglas and the regional hospital where all three children would be checked out. Although Jake knew he'd been on more dangerous rescue missions before, none had ever drained him as badly as this one.

It was finding Samantha that had shook him in a way no other operation ever had.

He lifted his arm just enough to brush a strand of short dark hair from her cheek. She slept soundly despite the noise of the rotors. She'd been so brave. As they'd waited out the storm, huddled around the warm stove, both she and Paul had told him how they'd come to be stranded at the bottom of the narrow fissure. She hadn't cried or given in to the fear he knew must be hovering just beneath the surface. And when the rescue team had finally arrived to take them off the mountain, she'd followed their orders exactly, without question, hesitation or argument. Jake had an idea that both she and Paul knew how badly they'd screwed up and were ready to make amends.

She was a child any man could be proud to claim as his own.

With that, his thoughts shifted to Ali, and he struggled with a myriad of conflicting emotions. How was a man supposed to react at discovering that the woman he loved had given birth to his child without his knowledge? Anger, excitement, fear, joy, regret— they all had a part to play in this drama. And sorting them out wasn't going to be easy.

Sam sighed and snuggled closer. A soft smile tugged at Jake's lips and again he brushed at her crop of soft hair. He realized at that moment there was one more overriding emotion vying for his attention. Love.

ALI STOOD ANXIOUSLY at the edge of the helicopter pad.

Though she'd been assured over the radio that all

three children were okay, she wouldn't be satisfied until she held her daughter in her arms.

The relief she'd felt when hearing that Sam was safe had drained the last of her reserved strength. Or so she'd thought. The day hadn't been over yet. Following John and Gail, she'd driven to Douglas, a trip that felt even longer than the one that morning.

Now, once again, she waited.

A member of the hospital staff stood beside her, keeping a firm but gentle hand on her arm as a team of nurses headed for the landing aircraft with a gurney. Jake was the first one off, and a small figure clung to him, her dark head resting against his shoulder and her arms wrapped around his neck.

"Jake! Sam!" Ali pulled away from the restraining hand and ran toward the large man holding her daughter.

Obviously hearing her mother's voice, Sam lifted and turned her head, then squirmed out of Jake's arms. Ali met her halfway across the landing pad and swept her into her arms with kisses, tears and a flood of relief.

"I was so worried about you. Are you okay?" Ali asked, examining her daughter with probing hands. "Are you hurt?"

Sam shook her head, the preadolescent tomboy dissolving into a little girl as she broke into tears. Ali drew her back into her arms, offering comfort with her touch and soft, soothing sounds whispered against the child's ear.

"She's fine, Ali," Jake reassured her. "A few cuts and bruises, that's all."

Ali smiled up at him and a fresh batch of tears slid down her face. "Thank you," she said, though she knew she could never thank him enough. Nothing could ever repay him for bringing her child back to her. *His* child. He must know by now, yet he said nothing. For that, too, she was grateful. "And the others?" she asked. "Paul and Brad? Are they okay?"

"Paul sprained his ankle," Jake said. "And it looks like Brad has a concussion, but I think he's going to be fine."

Ali nodded, closed her eyes and tightened her hold on Sam. She never wanted to come this close to losing her daughter again. Never.

"Ms. Kendrick," a male voice said beside her.

She looked up at an awkward young man in white who had brought a wheelchair beside them. "Yes?"

"Uh, I need to take her inside."

Ali wasn't ready to let go of her daughter, not even for the medical staff. She started to shake her head and tell him she'd take Sam in, but Jake's large hand on Ali's shoulder stopped her.

"You can go along," he said. "But let him take her in the chair. It's hospital policy, and she needs to be looked at by a doctor."

"Of course you can stay with her," the young man offered hurriedly.

Ali threw a glance at Jake, who nodded. Reluctantly, she helped Sam into the chair. Sam smiled bravely but never let go of Ali's hand as they headed into the emergency room and through the doors leading to the examination area. Suddenly, Ali realized Jake was no longer at her side. Stopping, she turned to see him standing beside the nurses' station.

"Aren't you coming?" she asked.

"You go ahead." He met her gaze, and a jolt of

certainty passed through her. He was giving her this time alone with Sam, maybe the last time the two of them would have before Jake claimed his daughter. "We'll talk later."

She hesitated, wanting him with her, but grateful, too, for these last moments when Sam would be all hers. Finally she nodded and let the nurse push Sam inside.

The doctors, evidently warned of their arrival, were ready and waiting for the three children who'd been lost for more than twelve hours in the Laramie Mountains. In Sam's case the examination was quick and painless. Ali stayed with her, standing next to the table the whole time. Sam was more subdued than usual, answering the doctor's questions politely and every few seconds darting glances at her mother, as if to make sure Ali was still in the room.

"Well, that's about it," the doctor said as she pulled off her latex gloves. "Besides a mild case of hypothermia, I'd say you're one lucky young lady."

"Yes, ma'am." Sam looked properly chastised, and Ali hid her smile. At the moment, she was just glad to have her daughter back alive and well. Sooner or later, though, Sam was going to have to face what she'd done, and obviously, the eleven-year-old was well aware of it.

"I'm going to send someone in to clean up those scratches," the doctor said, "then ask the nurse to get something warm in you, soup or hot chocolate. After that, you're free to go home." With a knowing smile to Ali, the doctor left.

Ali wrapped an arm around Sam's shoulder but neither of them spoke. For the moment, it was just so wonderful to have her daughter close again. A few minutes later, the same male nurse who'd wheeled Sam into the room arrived to clean and dress her scratches. She sat through the whole thing stoically, even though Ali could see an occasional suppressed wince.

When he finished, the young man said, "Since I think your mom probably has some paperwork to take care of, how about if I go get your friend Paul, and the three of us go down to the cafeteria to get a little something to eat?" He looked at Ali for approval. "They make a killer chicken noodle soup."

Sam threw a questioning look at Ali, who nodded reluctantly, still hating to let Sam out of her sight. "Go ahead," she answered. "But be careful."

"Don't worry, Mom," Sam said brightly. "Nothing's gonna happen to me in the hospital cafeteria."

And Ali knew she had her preadolescent tomboy back.

JAKE WATCHED THE GROUP of frazzled parents and mollified children disappear behind the emergency room doors, and he suddenly felt very much alone. It didn't make any sense, but for a while today he'd felt like a father. Then reality had set in. The helicopter had landed, and Ali had claimed her daughter.

He didn't belong here, and *they* didn't belong to him.

He wandered back to the empty waiting room with his hands in his pockets, unsure what to do next. Until he knew whether the doctors were going to keep the kids overnight, or whether Ali was in any condition to drive back to Lightning Creek, he couldn't leave. Yet he didn't know if he wanted to face her again right away, now that he knew about Sam. Or if Ali even wanted him here. Sooner or later they were going to have to discuss Sam, and he didn't know if either of them was up for that tonight. They were both too frayed, too on edge to think clearly.

"Excuse me," said the nurse behind the desk. "Mr. Merrill."

"Yes?" He walked over to her, grateful for anything to distract him from his tumultuous thoughts.

"The pilot who flew you in asked me to tell you he had to get back." She smiled shyly. "He said he thought you could get another ride back to Esterbrook or wherever."

"Sure." So much for distractions. Or an escape route. "Thanks." Jake started to walk away.

"Also," she said, stopping him, "he told me what you did for those kids. How you climbed into that canyon during a storm." He turned back to look at her, and she blushed. "He said you saved the lives of your daughter and her friends."

He thought about correcting her misconception about his and Sam's relationship, but didn't. He couldn't pretend Sam wasn't his, nor could he admit he hadn't known of her existence until a few hours ago. He gave the nurse a tight smile. "It's what I do. Just like this—" he made a sweeping gesture to encompass the hospital "—is what you do."

Her smile broadened but she didn't look convinced. Turning away from her, he retreated to the waiting room, her words like a steady drumming in his head. She had assumed that Sam was his daughter, either that or the pilot had made the leap. Evidently Jake wasn't the only one who just had to look at Sam to know she was his.

Settling into a hard plastic chair, he resigned himself to staying put for a while. Whether they were ready or not, he and Ali were going to have to talk about Sam.

*Sooner* rather than later.

# CHAPTER NINE

A HALF HOUR LATER, Jake stood as Ali entered the waiting room, folding his arms across his chest to keep himself from pulling her into them. She looked exhausted, both physically and emotionally. Her eyes were red-rimmed and there were lines of fatigue around her mouth. Yet she'd never looked more beautiful or desirable to him. Although it seemed an eternity ago, it had only been this morning when he'd held her in his arms. Now things had shifted between them, and he didn't know whether it was for the better or worse.

"Where's Samantha?" he asked.

Ali gave him a tight smile. "The nurse took her and Paul down to feed them soup. I guess they're both slightly hypothermic."

"But the doctors aren't keeping the kids overnight, are they?"

"No. Evidently it's not necessary. The doctor thought it was more important for them to spend the night in their own beds." Ali wrapped her arms around herself, and Jake thought how odd the two of them must look. They stood like mirror images, both afraid to reach out and offer or receive comfort from the other.

Jake shoved his hands into the back pockets of his jeans. "Did you drive up in my Jeep?"

She nodded. "Gail and John wanted me to come with them. But I couldn't."

He thought he understood. It was for the same reason he hadn't wanted to intrude on Ali and Sam in the examining room. What Ali had faced today, the close call that had almost torn her child from her...well, that wasn't something you could share.

"I'll drive you and Sam back to Lightning Creek," he said. "When you're ready to go."

"I can go with Gail and John," she told him.

"I'll take you."

He expected her to argue with him. Instead she nodded and said, "Thank you."

He realized she knew as well as he that before the night was over, there were things they needed to resolve. Motioning toward the bank of chairs, he said, "You look exhausted. Come on and sit down."

Again she nodded, and he led her over to the chairs. They both sat, keeping one seat between them. An awkward silence followed. Even though they both knew they needed to talk about Sam, neither was ready. Nor was this the time or place. Yet the subject hung between them, like the dark clouds of the storm.

Finally, Ali said, "Did Sam or Paul tell you anything?" There was still a faint tremor in her voice that tugged at his heart. "What they were doing wandering around that mountain at night? Or why?"

Jake settled uncomfortably on the wobbly plastic, crossing his legs with a hand on one knee, wishing he had the right to comfort her. "Seems Sam and Paul were trying to teach their new friend Brad a lesson."

"A lesson?"

"Well, that's not how they phrased it," he clarified, pleased at least to be talking about a semi-safe topic. "Evidently, Brad is a bit of a braggart just like that other boy at the camp said. His father's very wealthy, and he didn't let the other kids forget it."

She nodded, encouraging him to go on.

"So Paul and Samantha came up with this plan. They told Brad the Legend of Chief Wild Foot."

She looked at him incredulously. "The what?"

He laughed lightly, the first time all day, and it felt good. "The Legend of Chief Wild Foot."

She started to say something, but Jake held up a hand to stop her. "Just wait," he said. "Let me finish. According to Sam, Chief Wild Foot was a wise old Indian who used to roam the Laramie Mountains and knew all of their secrets—including the location of the hidden gold of the Shoshone Indians."

"Hidden gold?"

Grinning, Jake continued, "One night, while Chief Wild Foot was performing a ceremonial joining with the Moon Goddess, several soldiers found and captured him. The soldiers demanded that Wild Foot tell them where the gold was hidden. When he refused, they killed him."

Ali blinked.

"Since then, for the past hundred years or so," Jake continued, "Chief Wild Foot has come back every full moon to haunt the north face of Laramie Peak and take his revenge on the white man."

Shaking her head, Ali said, "I don't think I've ever heard that particular story."

Jake grinned. "That's because Sam made it up. Very creative, don't you think?"

Ali frowned. Obviously right now wasn't the time to point out the more creative aspects of her daughter's latest escapade.

"Anyway," Jake continued, "Sam and Paul talked Brad into going with them to see the ghost of Wild Foot. They admitted that Brad wanted nothing to do with it at first. He claimed not to believe them. But they used a time-honored method to get him to go along."

"They dared him?"

"Something like that. They accused him of being afraid."

"Boy, are those two in trouble." Ali looked miffed, and it hit Jake that this woman was a mother. Intellectually he'd known that for the last twelve hours, but somehow, sitting here watching her get angry with her daughter brought the reality home. She'd raised this child, loved and nourished her, but disciplined and punished her, as well. She'd done all the things he never had, and what right did he have to step in now and expect to don the role of Sam's father?

"So how did they end up on that cliff?" she asked, interrupting his thoughts.

"Well, that's the really scary part. They were headed for the sacred stone of Chief Wild Foot—"

"Hah!" She rolled her eyes skyward.

He continued, despite the urge to pull her into his arms and make her see the humorous side of this long, harrowing day. "When they ran into a real live mountain lion, they got spooked, started to run and ended up on top of that bluff on some very soft ground.

"It gave way beneath them, and Brad fell first, hitting his head on the way down. Paul tried to grab him and sprained his ankle in the process. They both ended up at the bottom of the crevice."

"And Sam?" Ali asked.

"According to Paul," Gail said from the doorway to the waiting room, "she climbed down to help them, and they all ended up stuck."

Ali rose and crossed the room to her friend and husband, who stood hand in hand. "Are you two okay?"

"We're fine," Gail said, releasing John's hand long enough to give Ali a brief hug. "We've been down in the cafeteria hearing the kids' story. I don't know whether to laugh, cry or wring their scrawny necks."

Ali smiled and it warmed Jake's heart, though he wished he'd been the one to draw it out of her.

"Well, I think the three of us need to sit down and talk about this, and come up with a comparable punishment for both of them," Ali said. "Something that will make them understand just how serious their little prank was."

"I agree," Gail said. "And—"

Suddenly there was a flurry of activity outside the emergency room door, and they all turned to see what was happening. Several cars had pulled up, along with a long black limousine. A uniformed driver was holding the limo's back door, and a man stepped out in a suit that screamed money, even if the vehicle he rode in hadn't. An entourage immediately closed around him, and he spoke a couple of words, then headed for the hospital entrance with two of the other men following. As the doors swished open, the three men strode inside.

The one in charge walked directly to the nurses' station. The other two men flanked him while throwing furtive glances around the room. "I'm Ted Gibbons," he said to the nurse on duty. "I was told you have my son Brad here."

"Oh, of course, Mr. Gibbons." The nurse looked a bit flustered. "The doctor is with him now."

"Please, I'd like to see him."

"Just a minute," she said, pushing away from the desk. "Let me check."

Gibbons stepped back from the station as the nurse got up and headed through the treatment area doors. He glanced around, nodded at the four of them in the waiting room entrance.

Jake tried to place the man. Ted Gibbons? The name was familiar, but Jake couldn't... Then it hit him. Ted Gibbons, founder and CEO of Millennium Corporation, an Internet software company that had skyrocketed to prominence in the last five years. The outstanding success of the company had been attributed to Gibbons himself, who was considered a genius on a level with Bill Gates. And almost as wealthy. The media hype surrounding the man had been intense, and evidently his son had bought into it.

The nurse returned and said, "The doctor will be right out."

"Is my boy okay?" There was an edge in Gibbons's voice, restraint or fear, Jake couldn't tell. "Can you tell me what happened?"

"I'm sorry, sir, the doctor—"

"Ms...." He glanced down at the woman's name tag. "Ms. Reynolds. I need to see my son. Please."

Jake stepped forward. "Excuse me, Mr. Gibbons."

The two men with Gibbons moved quickly to his side, but stopped their advance when Gibbons held up his hand. "What is it?"

"I'm Jake Merrill." He extended his hand. "I was with Brad in the helicopter."

"Mr. Gibbons," the nurse said, "this is the man who saved your son's life."

Gibbons glanced from the nurse to Jake and then took Jake's offered hand. "I guess I owe you, then."

"No, sir," Jake responded. "My daughter was out there, as well."

The man nodded, the anguish in his eyes almost palpable. Underneath the veneer of wealth, he was just another father who loved his son. "What happened out there?"

"He hit his head when he fell, but regained consciousness in the helicopter. The paramedics seemed to think he had a minor concussion. I'm no doctor, but for what it's worth, I think Brad is going to be all right."

Relief flooded the man's face. "Thank you. I appreciate the information."

"Why don't you have a seat, Mr. Gibbons?" the nurse said. "Dr. Wills promised he'd be out in just a minute."

Gibbons nodded and started toward a row of plastic chairs.

"There he is," came a female voice from behind them.

Jake turned, but before he could further react, Gibbons's two goons had intercepted the woman and cameraman behind her.

"Mr. Gibbons," she called, trying to push past the men, "can you give us a statement about your son?"

Without waiting to hear Gibbons's reply, Jake took Ali's arm and led her through the treatment room doors.

"Come on," he said. "Let's find Sam and get out of here." The last thing he wanted was a run-in with the news media. Let the likes of Ted Gibbons deal with them.

THE RIDE HOME WAS QUIET.

Neither Ali nor Jake spoke, and Sam fell asleep almost immediately with her head on Ali's lap. Ali kept a hand on the sleeping child, tucking the blanket around her tighter, brushing a strand of hair away from her cheek, or just rubbing her back. She needed to touch her child, to reassure them both that she was safe.

When they finally pulled into her yard, Ali sighed with relief.

Jake parked and came around and opened her door. Reaching inside, he lifted Sam as if she weighed nothing. As she'd done when they climbed off the helicopter together, Sam wrapped her arms around him without waking. It was as if at some level Sam knew he was her father. Ali followed them to her front door, and Jake stepped back to let her open it. Walking inside, she led him to Sam's room and motioned for him to lay her on the bed. He took a step back, shoving his hands into his back pockets.

"I'll wait outside," he said in a quiet voice.

"Thank you," Ali replied, grateful for the help. She wasn't sure she could have made the drive without him tonight. Not after everything that had happened. "It'll just take me a minute to get her tucked in."

He waited a moment and said, "You know we need to talk, Ali."

She bit her lip and nodded. "Yes, I know."

The last of the afternoon light had faded into night when Ali finally joined Jake on her front porch. He stood with his arms crossed, staring into the early darkness beyond the house. Though she knew he'd heard her come outside, he didn't turn around. Feeling awkward, she wrapped her arms around her waist and waited for him to say something.

So much had happened in the last twenty-four hours. It was difficult to believe that this time yesterday they were sitting on another front porch, a couple of hours south of here, contemplating making love. Things felt different between them now—awkward and uncertain—yet nothing had changed. Except for Jake finding out about Sam. Ali closed her eyes briefly and wondered who she was trying to kid.

Everything had changed.

"Were you going to tell me about her?" he asked in a tight voice.

Opening her eyes, she looked at him. She had to give him credit for holding back this long, for not asking her earlier about Sam. Bracing herself against his anger, she moved forward to stand a few feet away from him at the railing. "I was planning on telling you yesterday. But then one thing led to another..."

He glanced sideways at her, and for one long, uncomfortable moment, their gazes locked. Ali's cheeks heated with the memory of how they'd spent the previous night, and she turned away to study the featureless yard as he'd done earlier.

"I was going to tell you this morning," she answered. "Before the call came from Gail. After that, all I could think about was finding Sam. Besides, I was afraid if I told you at that point, it would make your job harder." She paused, dropping her gaze to her hands, which gripped the painted wood. "I wasn't going to let you go back to Colorado without knowing."

The silence that followed seemed to stretch on forever.

"It was her eyes that gave it away," he said finally. "It's like looking into a mirror." He laughed briefly, almost bitterly, and shook his head. "Ever since the moment I realized she was my daughter, I've been trying to be angry with you. Trying to blame you for not telling me about her." He sighed, and she sensed the anger drain out of him. "But to tell the truth, it's myself I'm angry at."

Running a hand through his hair, he turned sideways to look at her. "It's my own fault I don't know her, that I've missed all those years."

Surprised, Ali looked up at him. Even in the darkness she could see the pain in his eyes. Of all the reactions she'd thought he might have upon learning he had an eleven-year-old daughter, this had never crossed her mind.

"I'm the one who left and never looked back." He let out another short, disgusted laugh. "I should have at least checked on you to find out if you were pregnant."

Ali turned away, not sure how to handle this.

She hadn't known what to expect when she told him about Sam, hadn't known how she wanted him to react. Ali had figured he would be angry with her for not telling him sooner, or for not making more of an effort to locate him. Instead, he was accepting the blame for not knowing about his daughter.

"What did you tell her about me?" he asked, jarring her from her uncomfortable thoughts.

She looked up at him and lifted her shoulders in a shrug. "Basically the truth. That when you and I broke up, I didn't know I was pregnant. By the time I found out, you'd left the state and I didn't know how to get hold of you." She paused, and in case he didn't understand her reasoning, added, "I didn't want her to grow up thinking her father didn't want her."

"I guess that was better."

"It was the truth." But she couldn't let him accept all the blame. Because of her anger, she'd never really tried to find him once she knew she was pregnant. "And I did it to protect her. Not you."

He ran his hand through his hair again, and she seemed to lose him for a moment as he retreated into his own thoughts. She realized this must be harder on him than her. At least she had always known about his and Sam's relationship. It was new territory for him, and very sudden.

"And now?" he asked.

"That's up to you, Jake." She crossed her arms against the sudden chill in the air. "She's your daughter, and I won't try to keep her from you."

He seemed to think about that for a bit, then moved to the steps and sat down. "She's a great kid."

"Yes, she is."

"She's got a lot of spunk. Without her, the Gibbons boy might not have made it. Paul said it was her idea to get him out of the wind and under that ledge. And they huddled around him all night to help keep him warm."

Even if that was the truth, Ali thought, he needed to realize and admit something else about Sam, as well. "If it weren't for Sam," Ali said evenly, "neither Paul nor the Gibbons boy would have been out on that mountain at night to begin with. Sam's an instigator.''

He looked up at her, his brow furrowed. ''What are you saying?''

She sighed and sat on the step, as well, though she kept to the far side, leaning against the opposite rail post. ''I just don't want you to get the wrong impression about Samantha. I love her desperately, but she's no angel.''

He shook his head. ''I don't expect or want her to be an angel.''

''Good,'' she said. ''Because I don't want you to hurt her later if she disappoints you.''

''I wouldn't—''

She held up a hand to cut him off. ''Don't make promises you're not sure you can keep, Jake. This is all as new to you as it's going to be to Sam. As I said, I won't keep her from you. But I won't let you hurt her, either.''

He stared at her for a long moment, a spark of irritation flaring in his eyes. Then he extinguished it. ''I understand.''

Ali took a deep breath, her heart pounding as if she'd just run a race. Risking her own heart with Jake was one thing, risking her daughter's was something else entirely. And yet, a niggling voice at the back of her mind reminded her, this man had saved Samantha's life. If it weren't for him, who knew if the kids would have been found? Yet Ali was treating him as if she expected him to hurt Sam, as if she still didn't trust him.

''So when are we going to tell her?'' he asked, bringing her out of her thoughts.

Ali considered that for a moment. "I'd like to tell her alone, if you don't mind."

When he just looked at her as if waiting for an explanation, she offered him one. "Sam likes you, but this is going to be a shock. I want to tell her and let her get used to the idea first." She clasped her hands around her knees, bracing herself against any objection he might come up with. "Then we'll take it from there."

He hesitated and turned to stare off in the distance again. Finally he took a deep breath and nodded his acquiescence. "You know her much better than I do. So if you think that's best, I'll go along with it. When are you going to tell her?"

"First thing in the morning." Ali had put this off too long already and was anxious to finally get it all out in the open.

"Okay," he said. "I'll tell you what I'll do. John offered to drive down with me to your cabin tomorrow. He'll bring back your car, and I'll head on back to Colorado from there. Will you be okay for a day without a car?"

"I'll call Gail if I need something."

"Good." He nodded. "I need to take care of a few things in Colorado, but I'll be back next weekend. Will that be enough time?"

Ali loosened her hold on her knees. "That will be fine."

For a moment she thought he was going to say something else. She felt the tension in him, the need to talk about other things left unsettled between them. Instead, he stood and brushed off his jeans. "I'm going to head on over to the Starlite Motel for the night, and I'll come back in the morning for my Jeep."

"No, take the Jeep." Ali stood, as well. "I won't need it. And it's quite a hike down the hill to town."

"I want you to have a vehicle in case of an emergency." He glanced back at the house. "In case you need anything for Sam in the middle of the night."

"If I have an emergency," she insisted, "I'll call." When he didn't seem convinced, she added, "I'd rather you weren't here in the morning, Jake."

He stared at her and then sighed. "Okay, Ali, we'll do this your way."

"Thank you."

Again she thought he was on the verge of saying something else and she held her breath. She knew there were other things they needed to discuss, things that concerned just the two of them and the night they'd spent in each other's arms. But she couldn't deal with it right now. She was so tired she could barely stand, let alone think clearly about her relationship with Jake Merrill. She had a hard-enough time doing that under the best of circumstances.

"Well, I guess I should call it a night," he said.

Both relieved and disappointed, and feeling foolish about both, she forced a smile. "It's been a long day."

"And I've got a long drive ahead of me tomorrow." He took a tentative step toward her, but she backed up. With a resigned sigh, he shoved his hands into his pockets. "Well, I'll see you both next Saturday, then. Say about ten. I'll plan to spend the whole day with Sam."

"That will be fine."

"Okay, have a good week." He backed toward the Jeep.

"You, too. Good night."

Finally he turned and started for his Jeep, stopping after a few steps to look back at Ali. "There's one other thing I need to ask you."

She stood there, waiting.

"What about us, Ali?" He took a few steps back toward her. "Where are we? I mean, did last night..." He frowned. "I just need to know where we stand."

Tears filled her eyes, and she brushed them impatiently aside. "I don't know, Jake," she said honestly, already missing him and wishing she could fall into his arms. "Right now, Sam is my priority. I just can't risk her being hurt."

His frown deepened and he turned his head to look away from her. "Okay, Ali, I'll accept that for now. But sooner or later, we're going to have to talk about what's between us." He met her gaze and held it. "Because whether you want to admit it or not, it's not just going to go away. Not for either of us."

Biting her bottom lip, she nodded, again holding back the tears.

"Go on now and get some sleep," he said, so gently that it almost broke her resolve to keep her distance from him. "I'll see you in a few days when we're both feeling a bit more normal." Again he started for his vehicle.

"Jake?"

He turned quickly. "Yeah."

"Thank you for saving Sam's life, for giving me back my daughter."

"She's my daughter, too, Ali."

She nodded. "I know."

He stood for a moment longer in the darkened yard, then silently climbed into his Jeep and drove away.

Ali remained where he'd left her, watching his retreating taillights.

Finally she headed back inside, closing and locking the front door behind her. She went directly to Sam's room. Without taking off her clothes, Ali lay down on the bed next to her daughter, pulled her into her arms and slept.

THE NEXT AFTERNOON Ali was getting the kennel ready for the return of her boarders when she heard a car pull up outside, followed by an excited bark. Smiling for the first time in what seemed like days, she headed out front. Gail stood next to her Bronco with Chester, who started for Ali the moment she stepped outside.

"Chester!" Sam burst from the house, and the shepherd changed directions midflight and raced off to greet her. She bent down, and the excited dog bounded into her arms, knocking her over backward.

"Calm down, you silly dog," Sam scolded affectionately. Chester replied by licking her face enthusiastically. "Stop that," she said, though she didn't loosen her hold on him or make any effort to turn her face away. "You're getting me all covered with dog spit."

Laughing, Ali crossed the yard to stand next to Gail.

"Thanks for bringing him home, Aunt Gail," Sam called.

"And for having John watch him all weekend," Ali reminded her daughter.

Sam stood, and Chester bounced up as well, barked once and skittered around her with his tail wagging like crazy. Sam giggled, her eyes never leaving the frolicking animal. "Yeah, and for watching him all weekend."

"You're welcome," Gail said.

Sam came over to them with Chester still prancing around her.

"So, how are you doing, kiddo?" Gail asked.

Sam threw a tortured look at her mother and said, "Okay, I guess."

"Uh-huh," Gail responded. "I guess that means you're grounded."

"For the whole summer."

"Is that all?" Gail planted her hands on her hips and looked thoughtful. "I was planning on grounding Paul for the rest of his life."

Sam's eyes widened. "Aunt Gail…"

Gail called up her best motherly voice and said, "You know, Sam, all three of you could have died out there. And although you and Paul got off easy, Brad Gibbons was seriously hurt."

Sam dropped her gaze to the ground while digging the toe of one sneaker into the dirt. Chester let out a soft canine whine but they all ignored him. "I know," Sam said.

"I expect you do." Gail softened her tone. "And that's why your mother and I agreed that you and Paul are only going to be grounded for the summer."

Sam looked from one woman to the other. "You mean you talked about it and decided together?"

"Of course we talked about it," Ali interjected. "What you did was very serious, and we want to make sure you both understand that."

"Does Paul have to work all summer, too?"

Gail nodded. "He has to work with his dad, just

like you're working here in the kennels with your mom."

"Boy," Sam said, looking dejected. "It's gonna be a crummy summer."

Ali forced back a smile. It was amazing how quickly kids recovered. Last night Sam had been a little girl in her arms, cold and frightened. Now, less than twenty-four hours later, she was again her usual self. "Don't forget you're both getting paid for your work," Ali reminded her.

"I don't get to keep the money."

"Sure you do," Ali said brightly. "It goes into your college fund."

Sam rolled her eyes. "Big deal."

"Okay, Samantha," Ali said. "Go on and finish cleaning out that last cage for me. Doc Martin will be here with the poodles anytime. Then you'll be done for the day."

As Ali watched her daughter head back to the kennel with her dog bouncing beside her, Gail said, "So, how's she doing really?"

Ali shrugged. "As well as can be expected, I guess. She woke up in the middle of the night crying. And you see how she is today, sullen, willful and more like a teenager than I'm ready for. But I expect she'll be okay in a few weeks. How about Paul?"

"About the same," Gail responded.

Ali smiled grimly. "I guess no one ever said raising kids was going to be easy."

"No, but I don't ever remember anyone warning me that it would be this hard, either."

Laughing, Ali motioned toward the house. "Come on and sit with me for a few minutes before you head back to Grand Central Station."

"So what about you?" Gail asked once they were settled on the top step of Ali's front porch. "How are you holding up?"

"About as well as can be expected. You?"

"Same." They both laughed, and Gail said, "So what's going on with Jake?"

Ali took a deep breath. "Well, you were right. Once he saw Sam, there wasn't much doubt that he was her father."

"How did he take it?"

"Pretty good, actually." She shrugged and leaned back against the rail support. "Do you want some coffee or something?"

Gail shook her head. "No, thanks. Was he upset?"

"Actually, he said he was angry with himself for not checking to see if I was pregnant."

"Wow." Gail raised her eyebrows. "That's a very mature response for a man."

Ali laughed. "Spoken like a true man-hater. You, the woman who's been married to the same man your entire life."

"Not my entire life," Gail objected. "Just most of it. Besides, just because I love John doesn't mean I'm blind to his faults. Sometimes it's like living with three little boys instead of two."

Ali shook her head, knowing Gail didn't mean a word of it. She adored her husband.

"So what now?" Gail asked.

"Jake's driving up from Colorado on Saturday to spend some time with her."

"Now I'm really impressed. Do you think he'll show?"

The thought of him not showing had crossed Ali's mind, but she'd decided to give him the benefit of the doubt. "I think so. He's not the same boy he was twelve years ago."

Gail nodded toward the barn-turned-kennel. "Have you told Sam yet?"

"This morning. Between the grounding and telling her about Jake, we had quite a session."

"Well, that's probably why she's so sullen."

"Could be," Ali agreed. "She was really quiet when I told her about Jake."

"What did you expect?"

"I don't know." Ali shrugged. "I guess I thought she'd be more excited. After all, it's not every day you learn who your father is."

"Give her time, Ali. She's just scared."

"You're probably right. I've decided to take off this week to spend time with her. I'm still boarding the poodles and have to check on the Randal mare who's about ready to foal, but that's it. Doc Martin has agreed to take care of any emergencies."

"That will be good for both of you." They sat in silence for a while, and Gail said, "So are you going to tell me what happened between you and Jake the other night?"

Ali had been hoping with all the commotion over the kids being lost and Sam meeting her father that Gail would let this particular aspect of the situation slide. She should have known better. "I don't know, Gail. It wasn't what I expected. To be honest, he wasn't what I expected."

Gail just looked at her, eyebrows arched.

"Don't look at me like that."

"Ali, you didn't sleep with him, did you?"

Ali felt her cheeks heat. "Gail, really…"

"You did, didn't you."

"What if I did?" Ali said defiantly.

Gail slapped a hand down on the step and shook her head. "I knew it. This whole thing was a bad idea."

"He saved our children's lives yesterday."

"One thing has nothing to do with the other," she insisted, and Ali knew she was right. "It's you I'm worried about."

"Please." Ali frowned. "I'm fine."

"Are you?"

"It was just sex, Gail. At my age I'm allowed that occasionally."

"Just tell me one more thing, Ali," Gail insisted, as if she hadn't heard a word Ali said. "Tell me you didn't fall in love with him again."

"Of course not," Ali answered automatically. "Aren't you listening to me? It was sex. That's all it was." But even as her friend looked at her with doubtful eyes, Ali wondered who she was trying to convince.

# CHAPTER TEN

JAKE MANAGED TO TIE THINGS up in Colorado much faster than he'd hoped.

The need to hurry had come over him on the long drive back from Wyoming when he'd decided that he didn't want to be a weekend dad. Not at first, anyway. He'd just discovered that he had a daughter and he wanted to get to know her. He wanted to find out everything about her, what movies she liked, her favorite flavor of ice cream, even what she did for her last birthday. Hell, he didn't even know the *date* of her birthday. The smallest details of her life suddenly seemed immensely important, because they were details he'd missed.

Then there was Ali.

If he tried telling himself that the only reason he wanted to return to Wyoming quickly was Sam, he'd be lying. Ali had put him off when he'd brought up the subject of their relationship. That was okay. She was under a lot of stress, and he'd give her a little time. But meanwhile, he wanted to see her again, hear her voice and smell the gentle fragrance that was uniquely hers.

He'd become a man obsessed with two women, and nothing could have kept him in Colorado one moment longer than necessary. So by Wednesday evening, he was back in Lightning Creek. He thought about driving directly to Ali's, and would have, if it wasn't for Sam. This would be their first meeting as father and daughter, and he didn't think it would be a good idea to surprise her. Instead, he checked into a motel and called from his room.

Thankfully, Ali answered the phone. "Hello."

"Ali, it's Jake."

"What's wrong?"

He smiled to himself at her assumption that something was wrong. "Nothing," he answered, knowing he'd given her plenty of reason to doubt him in the past. It was going to take time to win her trust again. "When's Sam's birthday?"

"Her birthday?"

"Yeah." Leaning back against the headboard, he stretched out his legs on the bed. "I realized the other day that I don't know when her birthday is."

She laughed softly into the phone. "April 11. So you're off the hook for a present this year."

"Damn, I guess I'll have to return the Porsche."

"This is Wyoming. It's a four-wheel-drive utility vehicle or nothing. And it might be a good idea to wait until she's a little older. Like sixteen."

"Right."

"So, is that why you called? To talk about Sam's birthday?"

"No." He realized it was the first time he'd talked to Ali on the phone since they were kids. "Do you remember when I used to sneak out at night and call you?"

He could almost see her roll her eyes, but there was a smile in her voice when she replied. "We talked for hours. Usually about nothing."

"Want to try it again?" He grinned. "I'm sure I can be more creative now."

"Really?" He heard the laughter—and something else, something suggestive and sexy—in her voice. "Have you had a lot of experience with that kind of phone talk?"

He laughed. "Yeah, I'm on a first-name basis with one-nine-hundred babes."

"You're nuts," she said, but he could hear the pleasure in her voice. "And this is costing you a fortune."

"Nope," he assured her. "It's a seventy-five-cents connection charge."

"What?" Her brow would be furrowed now, trying to figure out what he was talking about.

"I'm here," he said.

"You're here? As...in town here?"

"Just checked into the Starlite Motel about an hour ago."

There was a long silence from the other end of the line.

"That's not exactly the reaction I expected," he teased. "Something more along the lines of 'forget the phone talk and come on over' would be preferable."

"Jake..."

"I'm kidding, Ali." That was only half-true. He hadn't planned on going over there tonight, but the more he talked to her, the more he liked the idea. "I want to come out in the morning, if that's okay." When she didn't answer right away, he added, "To see Sam, of course. But if that's not going to work, I could—"

"No," she said. "That's fine. Tomorrow's as good

a day as any. You just surprised me, that's all. I wasn't expecting you until Saturday.''

"I know." He shrugged, though she couldn't see him. "I got things taken care of faster than I thought in Colorado.''

Again he heard the hesitation at the other end of the line. "What things?''

He hesitated. He'd planned to tell her all this in person, but it was too late now. He'd more or less let the cat out of the bag. "Ali, I'm not going back to Colorado right away. I've decided to stay here for the summer. Spend more time with Sam.'' *And you.*

It was evidently his night for rendering her speechless. "Ali? Are you still there?''

"Uh, yes. I just don't know what to say. What about your job?''

"I took a leave of absence.''

"Can you do that?''

"I did it, Ali. I've missed eleven years of Sam's life.'' He was surprised at the vehemence in his voice. "I can afford to spend a summer with her.'' He took a breath and a moment to calm down a bit. "Now, tell me about Sam. How did she take the news?''

Ali hesitated. "She's been kind of quiet about it, which isn't like her. But I imagine it was a shock.''

"Would you rather I wait until Saturday to come over?'' It wasn't his first choice, but if it would be easier on Sam, he'd do it.

"No,'' she answered thoughtfully. "Waiting to see you might be part of the problem. So I think the sooner we get this over with, the better.''

Jake took a deep breath, relieved. He, too, had felt the strain of waiting. "All right then, I should probably let you go. Is ten tomorrow okay?''

"It's fine. But, Jake, where are you going to stay this summer?"

"I've talked to the manager here and he's given me a monthly rate."

There was another long pause from the other end of the line before she said, "There's no need for that. You can stay here."

That was about the last thing he'd expected. "Ali, as much as I'd like to take you up on that, do you think it's such a good idea with Sam around?"

She laughed. "No. I didn't mean here in the house. You can stay in the kennel."

It was his turn to be speechless. "Well, I appreciate the offer," he said at last, "but I really think a motel would be more comfortable."

"I'm sorry." Again she laughed, and it did funny things to his insides. "I guess I'm a little out of it tonight. When I restructured the old barn to turn it into a kennel, I had the loft made into a small apartment in case I ever got to the point where I needed to hire help." She hesitated, maybe trying to gauge his response across the phone line. "It's not much, but it's clean and free and...yours if you want it."

Jake smiled, thinking this was working out better than he'd dared hope. Spending the summer with Ali and Sam, being close enough to see them day and night. What more could he ask for? "Well now," he said. "That sounds like an offer I can't refuse. I guess I'm just going to have to take you up on it."

ALI TOLD SAM AS SOON AS she woke up the next morning about Jake coming over. From that point on, it was impossible to get the eleven-year-old to do anything. She bounced from one thing to the next, excited and probably nervous. Ali understood all too well; she had her own feelings about Jake to deal with, including whether it had been a good idea to offer him the loft apartment. It made a lot of sense from a practical point of view. Why should he spend the money on a motel room when she had a perfectly nice, nearly brand-new, empty apartment just sitting there? And having him around for the entire summer wasn't an unpleasant thought, either. He and Sam could really get to know each other. And, she had to admit, she liked the idea for herself, as well.

He showed up a few minutes early.

Ali and Sam were both working in the kennel when Chester gave a warning bark and took off for the yard. Ali glanced at her daughter, who gave her a nervous smile.

Holding out her hand, Ali said, "Come on, sweetie. Let's go meet your dad." Sam took her hand and they went outside together.

Chester had acted as the advance greeting committee, and Jake had already won the shepherd's heart by scratching him enthusiastically behind the ears.

"Great dog," he called. Standing, he gave Chester a slap on the rump. "Go on, now."

Ali squeezed Sam's hand, and for once she didn't pull away. Jake seemed hesitant as well, standing next to the vehicle for a few moments before walking toward them. With a little tug on Samantha's hand, Ali met him halfway.

"Hello, Ali. Sam?" Ali heard the question in his voice. He was as nervous about this as the two of them.

"Hi, Jake." Ali smiled, trying to put them all at ease.

Sam had other ideas. "Are you really my dad?" she asked bluntly.

Jake looked momentarily taken aback and glanced at Ali for guidance, then turned back to their daughter. "Yeah. I'm really your dad. How do you feel about that?"

Sam shrugged. "It's okay, I guess."

Again he looked at Ali, who hadn't the faintest idea how to help him with this. It was new to her as well. Visibly taking a deep breath, he squatted down in front of the eleven-year-old. "I have to tell you something, Sam."

She didn't look overly eager to hear whatever it was he had to say, but he pressed on, anyway. "I'm new at this dad stuff." He ran a hand down his face, rubbing at his chin for a moment. "In fact, I don't have the faintest idea how to be a father. Do you think you can help me out here?"

She stared at him for what seemed like an eternity, then she gave him a crooked smile and lifted her shoulders in another shrug. "Don't worry. It's not so hard. Besides, I've had lots of experience being a daughter."

THE DAY WENT BETTER than Ali had expected, better than she'd dared hope.

After the initial awkwardness, Sam and Jake had hit if off amazingly well. He helped her finish her morning chores in the kennel, something Ali decided to allow this one time. She didn't want Sam thinking she could get around her punishment by letting Jake do her work, but today was a special occasion. And they all needed to make allowances. Besides, it was a good opportunity for father and daughter to get to know each other.

Ali still had the pair of boarding poodles, but Sam was responsible for their basic care. She fed them, cleaned their cage, and twice a day took them out for exercise in the large fenced run, which had been specifically designed for that purpose.

A little before noon, Ali heard Chester's enthusiastic barking and stepped outside to see what was going on. Jake and Sam were inside the run with the two poodles, who were cavorting like puppies, showing off or possibly teasing the oversize shepherd, who was safely locked outside their fenced area. But it was Jake and Sam who held Ali's attention. The man and the child, in some ways so physically alike it took her breath away, were rolling on the ground amid giggles and miniature canines jumping and yapping at them.

Ali's chest tightened, and a rush of tears stung her eyes.

For years she'd told herself that this was what she wanted, what was missing from her life. A man to be a father to her daughter, someone who would care for Sam as much as she did. She'd just never expected it to be Jake. A man she could love again without half trying. A man she still couldn't bring herself to trust with her heart. Or her daughter's. He'd walked away from them once before. How could she ever be sure he wouldn't do the same again?

She closed her eyes briefly and shook off the disturbing thoughts. It was too soon, too early to make any judgments. To decide now that Jake was the father Sam needed could be a devastating mistake. He'd known about Sam for less than a week and had spent a few hours with her on the mountain and a couple more this morning. They needed time before any of them knew where this new relationship was going. As for Ali's feelings about Jake, she couldn't let her emotions overrule her common sense. She'd made that mistake once before and couldn't afford to do the same again.

Steeling herself against the picture of Sam and Jake together, Ali walked over to the run and put a soothing hand on Chester's head. The big dog looked up at her with pleading eyes and lolling tongue.

"Sorry, big boy, I can't let you in," she said, scratching him behind the ears. "You're just too much for those little guys."

"Hey, Mom," Sam called, bouncing up and heading for the fence where Ali stood. "We're exercising the poodles."

"I can see that," Ali said with a grin. "And getting filthy in the process."

Sam grinned, knowing her mother didn't really care about things like that.

"I have to go check on the Randal mare again. Will you two be okay here alone?" Earlier in the week she'd taken Sam with her to check on the mare, who was about ready to foal. "Or do you want to come?"

"We'll stay here." Sam threw a look at Jake. Although she had been excited about the impending birth a couple of days ago, she seemed more than willing to let her mother go off alone today. "Won't we, Jake?"

Jake ambled to his feet, looking a bit tousled but incredibly sexy. "Sure, we'll manage. Besides, I noticed your fence out by the front gate was down."

Ali's cheeks heated in embarrassment. She preferred to keep things in order and didn't like getting caught with something left undone. "I haven't gotten around to fixing it." There just never seemed to be enough hours in the day.

"I'd be glad to take care of it for you," he said, dropping an affectionate hand to Sam's shoulder. "I thought since I helped Sam with her chores this morning, she could help me repair the fence this afternoon."

"Cool," Sam said, looking at her father with adoring eyes.

Ali felt another twinge of unease about how quickly her daughter had become attached to this man, but she forced a smile. "Great," she said, though she wanted to decline his offer.

In a matter of a few hours Jake had managed to insert himself into Sam's life, and it frightened Ali more than she wanted to admit. She didn't want either herself or Sam to start depending on him. But refusing to let him mend a broken fence would be childish and rude. "Sam can show you where we keep the tools."

"Sure. Come on, Jake." Taking his hand, Sam started toward the barn.

As Ali watched them, she suddenly didn't want to leave. A part of her wanted to snatch up her daughter and take her away, while another side of her wanted to join their play and work on the fence. Instead, she called, "And don't forget to spend some time with Chester, Sam. He's a little jealous of the poodles."

"Okay, Mom."

"I'll only be gone an hour or so," Ali added. "There's sandwich meat in the refrigerator if you get hungry."

Sam turned and rolled her eyes. "It's okay, Mom. We'll be fine."

Ali's cheeks heated. Her daughter knew her too well. And she suspected they would be fine. On the other hand, she wasn't at all sure how *she* was going to survive this. How she was going to continue seeing Jake day after day without losing her heart.

DINNER WAS A SIMPLE AFFAIR.

Ali had stopped at the grocery store on the way back from the Randals' ranch and picked up ground beef and all the accompaniments for a barbecue. She soon discovered that despite Jake's claim to only know how to cook breakfast, he was also pretty good over a grill. While he tended the hamburgers, Ali made potato salad, a tray of garnishes, and sweetened iced tea—compliments of her Georgia upbringing. Sam ran between the two of them, carrying food back and forth and delivering messages.

Finally they settled down at the picnic table on the back porch, with Chester at Sam's feet, watching hopefully for her to dole out scraps. After the first bite of her sandwich, Sam exclaimed that Jake's hamburgers were absolutely the best she'd ever tasted. For the rest of the meal she talked nonstop, telling Ali all about mending the front fence as if it were the most interesting topic ever. She also wanted a report on the pregnant mare, who was still a week or more away from delivering.

Ali smiled indulgently, knowing Sam was wound-up after her first day with her father. She was glad Jake had seen enough of Sam to know that she wasn't usually this high-strung. Then Sam blew that thought away with her next question.

"Jake," she said thoughtfully as they were finishing their meal, "are you gonna marry my mom?"

Jake nearly dropped his glass of tea. "Well, I..."

"Samantha, what kind of question is that?" Ali demanded, a flush of embarrassment touching her cheeks.

The picture of innocence, Sam said, "I just always wanted a *real* dad."

Jake, who'd recovered quickly, said, "Well, now you have one."

"Yeah, but it won't be the same if you don't live here," Sam insisted. "You know, like Uncle John lives with Aunt Gail."

"Sam," Ali interrupted. "That's enough."

"What'd I say?"

Ali threw an apologetic look at Jake before turning back to her daughter. "You know exactly what you said, and *I* know what you're trying to do."

Sam gave her a crooked frown. "Well, it was worth a try. I mean, I just thought it would be nice to have a *normal* family. I wouldn't even mind a baby brother."

"Sam..." Ali put a warning in her voice, while wishing the floor would just open up and swallow her whole.

"Okay, Mom." Sam looked dejected, for Jake's sake no doubt. She knew Ali had long ago ceased to fall for her attempts at parent psychology to manipulate her mother.

"I've got an idea," Jake said, changing the subject abruptly. "How about if we go in to town for some ice cream?"

"I can't," Sam answered sullenly with a furtive glance at her mother. "I'm grounded."

Ali bit her lip to keep from laughing at her daughter. What an actress! Jake, too, seemed to understand that this was an act—and a test—for his benefit. He threw Ali a questioning glance, and she nodded slightly.

"Well, I think we can forget about the grounding for one night," he said. "After all, it's not every day you get a *real* dad. What do you think, Mom?"

Ali pretended to consider the idea for a moment, then said, "Okay, this one time, since it's a special occasion. But we're not going to make a habit of this, Sam. Jake's going to be here all summer, and I don't want to hear pleading every night for the next few weeks."

"I won't ask again," Sam said, brightening almost instantly. "I promise. Just tonight."

"Okay, then." Ali stood and started picking up the dishes. "You two go on. I'll stay and clean up."

"Come on, Mom," Sam insisted. "You come, too."

"Yeah, Mom, come with us," Jake added, giving her a smile that made her heart beat a little faster.

Ali threw him a mock frown. "It will be good for the two of you to spend a little time alone."

"We've been alone all day." Sam sounded disgusted.

Suppressing a grin, Ali said, "Well, you're going to be alone again if you want ice cream tonight. I've got to clean up the kitchen and check on the animals." Besides, she wasn't quite ready for a cozy little family trip into town. Things were already moving too fast, and she was losing control. Of what, she wasn't sure. Sam? Jake? Their relationship, maybe? Or her own feelings about all of the above?

Sam looked ready to argue further, but Jake ran interference by saying, "Come on, sport. Let's leave your mom to the dishes. We'll get her to join us on another night.''

Ali didn't want to point out that they'd just agreed this was a one-night deal. That would just restart the whole discussion about her going all over again. So she let it slide, and once they were gone, she took a deep breath and sat back down at the picnic table for a moment. This really was going to be a tough summer, with Sam playing her against Jake, and the two of them worming their way past Ali's resistance. Then there was the problem of Jake himself. Putting aside her feelings for him wasn't going to be as easy as she'd hoped.

She'd just finished loading the dishwasher when she heard car doors slam outside. That was fast, she thought, glancing at the wall clock. They'd only been gone fifteen minutes. She hoped they didn't have a problem.

Heading toward the front of the house, she pushed through the screen door, stepped out onto her porch and stopped dead in her tracks.

''Well, are you just going to stand there and gape, young lady?''

''Dad?''

''Come give your old man a kiss.'' Her father reached her and wrapped her in his bearlike arms before she could blink. ''How's my favorite daughter?'' he said, hugging her tightly. ''Still intent on staying in this godforsaken country?''

''Now, Charles,'' said Margaret Kendrick, gingerly climbing the steps behind him. ''Don't start. And it's my turn for a hug.''

With a huge smile and one final squeeze, Charles released her. ''We can't forget your mother.''

"How are you, darling?" Margaret asked, stepping into her daughter's embrace. Her greeting was gentler, but no less loving than her husband's.

"Fine, Mom." Ali held on a little longer than necessary, then pulled back to look at her glamorous mother in a Chanel suit. "What *are* you two doing here?"

"What are we doing here?" Charles Kendrick boomed. "The better question is why weren't we here sooner? Which we would have been, if we didn't have to hear from your friend Gail about our one-and-only granddaughter being lost in the Laramie Mountains."

"Gail?"

"Your mother called her a couple of nights ago to see if there was anything special you wanted for your birthday next month. Instead, Gail told her about Sam."

"Now, Charles—" Margaret started.

"Where is Samantha, anyway?" he asked, ignoring his wife and glancing around the yard. "And why didn't you call us?"

"Charles, you promised."

"I only promised I wouldn't give the girl a hard time, I didn't say I wouldn't ask her a simple question. After all, it's our grandchild we're talking about here."

"You know," Margaret began, "that's just like you to twist things around."

"Wait a minute," Ali said, holding up both hands to quiet her parents. "You're here because of the incident in the mountains last weekend?"

"Why else, darling?" Margaret looked at Ali as if she should know better than to ask such a ridiculous question. "We were worried."

Ali shook her head and laughed lightly. She might not always see things the same way as her parents—like her mother traveling to the ranch country of Wyoming in a thirteen-hundred-dollar suit—but she could always depend on them. And she loved them dearly. "Sam's fine, Mom. You should have just called."

"That's what I told her," Charles said, frowning at his wife.

"If we had called," Margaret objected, not the least disturbed by what she would have called her husband's lack of manners, "you would have told us that everything was just fine and that we shouldn't bother to come out here."

Ali couldn't argue with her. That would have been exactly what she'd have told them.

"I wanted to see for myself," Margaret added before Ali could say anything.

"Hah!" Charles said. "She just wanted an excuse to see her grandbaby."

"And you didn't?" his wife challenged.

Ali grinned and again held up her hands to silence them. "Well, I'm glad you're here. Even if Sam is fine. And she'll be thrilled to see you both."

"So, where is she?" Charles demanded.

Ali hesitated and bit her lip. They couldn't have picked a worse time to show up on her doorstep if they'd planned it. But there was no point in putting off the inevitable any longer than necessary. "She's in town getting ice cream. They should be back soon."

"They?" her mother said, cocking her head sideways.

Ali nodded. "Jake took her. Jake Merrill."

"And who is this Jake Merrill?" her father demanded, drawing Jake's name out with a scowl.

"Oh, you remember, Charles," Margaret said, a sudden twinkle in her eyes. "Gail mentioned him. He's the man who rescued Samantha and the other two children from the mountain. Isn't that right, Alison?"

"Yes, Mom, that was Jake."

"Well, now," Margaret crooned. "He's here. Isn't that interesting."

"I don't see what's so interesting about it," Charles said grumpily.

"You wouldn't, dear."

"I'm hear to see my granddaughter," Charles complained, "and she's off having ice cream with some mountain climber."

"Jake's not just some mountain climber, Dad." Ali knew this was going to be bad. Her father was used to being in charge and tended to forget that Margaret and Ali weren't his employees and subject to his demands. She could count on her mother to keep him in line, but only after he'd bellowed and snorted like an angry bull.

"Of course he isn't, dear." Her mother patted Ali's hand and glared at her husband. "So, is there something you want to tell us?"

"What could she possibly have to tell us?" Charles demanded.

"Well, Dad, Mom's right. There is something you should know about Jake." Turning to her mother, she added quickly, "But it's not what you think, Mom." Of course, that wasn't entirely true. Again Ali hesitated, knowing her father wasn't going to like this.

"You see, Dad," she said. "Jake is Samantha's father."

# CHAPTER ELEVEN

"So you see," Jake said patiently to his newly found eleven-year-old daughter, "that's why your mom and I aren't going to get married. At least not now."

"But you might sometime."

He shook his head, thinking this parenting thing was a lot harder than he would have thought. "I don't know, Sam. We just never really talked about it."

"But you *could* talk about it."

"It's not that simple. People don't just get married. They have to be in love and want to spend the rest of their lives together." He felt for sure he'd already said these exact words and was beginning to sound like a broken record. But then, she kept asking the same thing. Different phrasing. Same question.

"But you like my mom, don't you?" she demanded.

"I like your mom very much, Samantha." He ran a hand through his hair and wished he'd insisted on Ali coming along. "It's just that there's a lot involved when a man and woman decide to get married."

She sat sullenly, and he wondered if any of his explanation was getting through to her. The interrogation had begun as soon as they'd left the house, continued through a double-dip cookies 'n' cream ice-cream cone, and didn't stop even as they headed back home. He'd realized very quickly that he wasn't nearly as adept at diverting unwanted lines of conversation as her mother. But Sam seemed so concerned about Ali and him getting married, and he couldn't quite figure out why.

If she were in school and around other kids, he might think someone was giving her a hard time about her parents not being married. But as far as he knew, she hadn't seen any other kids since the camping trip. Besides, he doubted whether that would be a problem, anyway. Nowadays one-parent families were common, and she'd been fatherless all her life. Besides, Sam was more likely to give another kid a black eye than take to heart any teasing about her parents' marital state.

No, something else was going on here.

"What's this really all about, Sam?" he asked, throwing her a quick sideways glance. "Why are you so concerned about your mother and I getting married? And don't give me that line about being a normal family. We both know there's no such thing."

Sam shrugged and dropped her chin to her chest.

For a moment, Jake thought she was playacting again. But then he saw the moisture in her eyes. Sam wasn't the type of kid who used tears to get her way. Manipulation, argument, badgering, maybe. But not tears. Not Ali's tomboy. Of course, he could be totally off base and not even know it. Pulling the Jeep to the side of the road, he shut off the engine and turned toward his daughter. His *daughter*. Just the word warmed his heart and made him smile.

"Okay, Sam, fess up." He reached over and tucked her short dark hair behind her ear. "What's bothering you?"

She shook her head and refused to look at him.

Women, he thought, he'd never understand them. "You know," he said, "you can tell me anything and it'll be just between the two of us."

"Is that true?"

"We can make it true. We'll make a father-daughter pact to keep each other's secrets."

"Promise?"

"You got it, sport. Now, tell me what's going on."

She visibly took a deep breath. "I just thought maybe, if you and my mom got married…well…"

A single tear dripped down her cheek, and she wiped at it impatiently.

"You thought what?" he prodded, knowing she wouldn't want her tears acknowledged. Not yet, anyway. Maybe in a few years.

"I just thought I could call you Dad instead of Jake."

Jake's heart seized up as if a giant fist had closed around it. "Oh, honey." He reached across the seat, pulled her onto his lap and wrapped his arms around her small frame. Suddenly it felt real. This was his child, and he was her father. "Your mom and I don't have to get married for that. I am your dad, and nothing would make me happier than for you to call me that right now."

She looked up at him with shiny eyes. "Really?"

"Really."

She broke into a grin. "And I can tell everyone I have a real dad and everything."

"We can take out an ad on a highway billboard if you want."

Sam laughed and wrapped her arms around his

neck, giving him an ice-cream-sweet kiss on the cheek. Again his heart did a funny little jig.

"Thanks, Dad." She grinned. "I can't wait."

"And no more talk about marriage," Jake said, though the idea of spending the rest of his life with Ali appealed to him in ways it never had before. "Your mom and I will deal with that in our own time, okay?"

"It's a deal, Dad."

As they drove the rest of the way home, Jake grinned, hoping it would always be so easy to please Sam. But somehow he didn't think so. Not with adolescence right around the corner. What a scary thought. He hadn't the first idea how to deal with a teenage daughter. Thank God for Ali. She, at least, had been there.

Just thinking of Ali, the woman who had given him this child, made him smile again. Maybe it was time the two of them had that talk, the one Ali had put off after bringing Sam back from the hospital. Hell, he'd given her a whole four days to get over the shock of things. That should be long enough. Tonight, after Sam went to bed, they'd talk. And who knew what else.

None of that was to be, however. When he drove into Ali's yard, there was a big white sedan parked in front, and a man and woman standing with Ali on the front porch.

"Who—" Jake began.

"That's my grandma and grandpa," Sam said excitedly. "They've come to see me." Almost before he could stop the Jeep, Sam was out the door and racing across the yard to fling herself in the large man's arms.

Jake got out of the vehicle much slower, approaching the group and instantly feeling like an intruder.

"How's my favorite granddaughter?" the big man said as Sam showered him with kisses.

She giggled and said, "I'm your *only* granddaughter."

"Is that right?" he said. "I could have sworn I had another couple around here somewhere. Maybe they were grandsons."

Sam giggled again and hugged him fiercely. "Nope. I'm the only one. And I'm a girl." Obviously this was a common exchange between the two.

"What about me?" the woman asked. "Don't I get a hug?"

The man passed Sam to the woman's outstretched arms. "Are you ever getting big," she said, not even flinching as the not-particularly-spotless child wrapped herself around the elegant pale pink suit.

"Hi, Grandma," Sam said, hugging her as fiercely as she had her grandfather. Then, when the woman put her down, Sam asked, "Did you bring me something?"

"Sam," Ali admonished.

The woman laughed and said, "Would I come all the way out here without bringing you something?"

Sam answered with a grin.

"It's in my suitcase," Margaret said, smiling.

"And I have a surprise for you, too." Sam dropped off the porch, grabbed Jake's hand and tugged him forward. "This is my dad." Everything seemed to come to a screeching halt, the smiles, the laughter. Everything except Sam's hopeful face and bright voice. "He's staying with us for the whole summer."

Again, no one said a word.

Then Ali stepped into the silence. "Mom, Dad, this is Jake Merrill, Samantha's father. Jake, my parents, Margaret and Charles Kendrick."

Jake almost didn't know how to respond, either to the open hostility in Charles's eyes or the cautious curiosity in Margaret's. Stepping forward, he nodded toward Margaret. "Mrs. Kendrick," he said, then extended his hand to Charles. "Mr. Kendrick."

For a moment Charles just stared at him, then his wife gave him a nudge with her elbow and said, "It's nice to meet you, Jake. May I call you Jake?"

Her husband finally took Jake's hand and shook it briefly, scowling the entire time.

"Yes, ma'am, you can," Jake answered. It was easy to see where Ali got her looks. She was a younger version of her mother, with the same thick auburn hair and eyes the color of autumn leaves.

"Then, please," she said. "I'm Margaret and this big oaf is Charles." Her husband glared at her, but she ignored him. "I hear we have you to thank for rescuing Samantha from the mountain last weekend."

"No, ma'am, there was a whole team that went in and carried out Sam and the other two children." He felt like an awkward schoolboy. "I just went in first and kept the kids calm while they waited."

"Whatever the case, as a grandmother, I thank you." Again, she nudged her husband. "We thank you."

Charles grunted and mumbled something Jake couldn't and probably didn't want to hear.

Jake stole a glance at Ali, who looked from her mother to her father. "Why don't we go inside." If her voice was a little too bright, no one seemed to notice.

"I'll get the luggage," Charles said, and headed toward the car.

With another glance at Ali, Jake followed him. "I'll help you."

"Come along, Samantha," Margaret said with an outstretched hand. "Why don't you show me your room."

Ali hung back, obviously unsure whether to follow her mother and Sam, or stay outside to make sure her father didn't bite off Jake's head. Despite the older man's claims of not needing help, Jake grabbed a couple of the bags, carried them to the house and set them in the front hallway next to the door. Then he returned to the porch. Without a word, Charles followed with the remaining bags and disappeared inside.

"Come with us, Jake," Ali said

He gave her a tight smile and backed up. "No, thanks, I think I'll call it a night. It's been a long day, and I need to get settled in." Nodding toward the house, he added, "Spend some time with your parents."

"Are you sure?" She looked relieved, though, and he couldn't blame her.

He nodded. "I'll see you in the morning. Tell Sam good-night for me."

"Okay." She took a step toward him and stopped. But her hands seemed to take on a life of their own, first clenched together, then fluttering free for a bit, until she finally wrapped them around her waist and said, "Good night, Jake."

"Good night, Ali," he said, letting her off the hook. He wished with everything in him that she'd kept walking until he had folded her into his arms.

But he was a fool for wishing for the impossible. Her family was here now; her true family.

With that thought circling in his mind, he headed for the converted barn and its apartment. But he couldn't go right inside. He needed time to think, and for that he required open space, not walls. Skirting the animal run, he came up behind the kennel to the west-facing fence, which separated the yard from Ali's open acreage. With one foot on the bottom rail and his arms on the top, he absently watched the daylight fade into the distant hills. Ali's big shepherd had followed and took up his own post next to Jake, his tail making slow sweeping motions in the dirt.

Who was he kidding? Jake thought.

For a while today, he'd almost felt he belonged here. To Ali and Sam. Helping his daughter with her chores and watching her gentle and efficient handling of the animals had been a pure joy. Her mother had taught her that, and it made him love Ali even more for her kindness and compassion and her easy manner with the child she'd raised alone.

Then fixing the fence.

He laughed bitterly and shook his head. For God's sake, it was only a damn fence, but it had felt like so much more at the time. As if he was mending something for all of them, within all of them. He'd felt— damn it, he'd felt like he'd belonged.

Then when Sam had asked to call him Dad, something inside him had come to life, and for a few minutes his soul had soared. He closed his eyes and fought down a surge of pain. In that moment, he'd lost his heart to the child as surely as he'd lost it to her mother twelve years ago. For the first time in his life he felt part of something, part of a family.

But he'd been a fool.

Jake didn't know the first thing about family. How to build one, or even how to be a part of one. He didn't belong here and never would. Just watching Sam with her grandparents had made Jake realize that. They were a family: Sam, Ali and her parents. And when Charles Kendrick had looked at Jake, his eyes filled with anger at the man who'd left his daughter alone and pregnant, Jake had understood that, too. Maybe he wouldn't have understood a few weeks ago, but he did now. He had a daughter, too, and he'd kill any man who did to her what he'd done to her mother.

With a sigh, he pushed away from the fence.

He'd told Ali and Sam he was staying for the summer, and he'd keep his word. After that, he'd head on back to the mountains of Colorado. He'd still be there for his daughter and see her as often as possible. And he'd be there for Ali, too, if she ever needed him. But he wouldn't forget his place again. Hell, he'd never belonged to anything or anyone in his life.

Why should that change now?

"I CAN'T BELIEVE YOU'RE letting him stay here," Charles said.

He'd waited until after Sam had gone to bed to voice his objections. But Ali had been aware since he'd first set eyes on Jake that her father was not happy about his presence in Lightning Creek. "I told you, Dad, he's staying in the apartment above the kennel."

"He's on your property."

"Keep your voice down, Charles," Margaret said. "This is not a discussion Samantha needs to hear."

"And that's another thing," he continued, though he did lower his voice. "How could you let him near my granddaughter?"

Ali felt her own temper rise. She'd faced off with her father before, and it was never a pretty sight. She could be as opinionated as he, and just as stubborn. "Samantha is *my* daughter, Dad. *And* Jake's. Not just your granddaughter."

"She's right, Charles," Margaret interceded. "We have no right to keep the two of them apart. Sam obviously thinks the world of Jake."

"Thank you, Mom," Ali said. "Sam has become attached to Jake very quickly." She sent a defiant look at her father. "And why not? He saved her life. But more than that, he loves her." She realized suddenly that it was true. This wasn't just some passing interest on Jake's part. He truly cared for Sam. Though how Ali knew that after one day, she couldn't say.

Charles let out a snort of disgust but kept his mouth shut when Margaret sent him a warning glare. Turning back to her daughter, she said, "But I am a little concerned about you, Alison."

Ali was concerned, too, but she wasn't going to admit it. Not to her mother, Gail or anyone else. What was between her and Jake was theirs alone. And if he broke her heart again, well, that was between them, as well. "I appreciate that, Mom, but I'm twenty-nine years old. I can take care of myself."

"That's true, darling. But it doesn't make you immune to being hurt."

What her mother said was true enough, and Ali realized Jake could hurt her now as badly as he'd hurt her twelve years ago. Maybe worse.

"Just be careful," her mother added, and kissed her on the cheek. After that, Margaret ushered Charles off to bed, leaving Ali to her thoughts.

As quietly as possible, Ali went out on her back porch and sat on the picnic table. The daytime warmth had faded with the sun, and the night was clear, a million stars brightening the dark sky. She shivered, thought about going back in for a sweater, but decided against it. She didn't want to wake Sam or encounter either of her parents again.

Funny, though, she was grateful to them for showing up unannounced. She wasn't prepared for company, and her father infuriated her sometimes, but with them came clarity. Earlier today, she'd been afraid of how fast things were moving between Jake and Sam, and of her own growing feelings for the man who'd once hurt her. Yet as soon as her father had attacked Jake and his presence here, she'd jumped to Jake's defense. She doubted whether her father would appreciate the irony of it, but it made her realize just how much Jake meant to her.

She loved him. Just as she always had.

Telling herself that their relationship was about sex had been a lie. She could have "sex" with any man. With Jake it had been more. And she couldn't bring herself to believe that he hadn't felt it, too. Twelve years ago he'd walked away from her, but he'd been young—they'd both been young—and he'd thought he was doing the right thing. He was wrong. And she was going to make sure that neither of them made that mistake again.

They belonged together. All three of them.

THE NEXT MORNING Ali sent Sam down to ask Jake up for breakfast.

When he sent back a message that he was on his way out to Lost Springs and would grab something in town, Ali decided she needed to go talk to him herself. Leaving Sam to help her grandmother find what there was to eat, Ali set off across the yard. Fortunately, Jake's Jeep was still parked outside, so she knew he hadn't left yet. She wasn't going to allow her parents' presence to keep him away from either her or Sam.

Letting herself inside the kennel, she glanced toward the door leading to the apartment. Chester lay in front of it, waiting patiently for the man. She walked over to the dog and crouched down to scratch his favorite spot. She wondered if she should knock. But approaching Jake in the apartment probably wasn't the smartest idea. Not with her parents up at the house and Sam likely to show up at any minute.

"Well, big boy," she said to the dog. "Just make sure he doesn't get past me."

Chester wagged his tail in response, and Ali went about her morning chores. She fed the poodles, who were being picked up today, and made sure Sam was taking care of the other cages and work areas the way she was supposed to. As for Jake, Ali heard him before she saw him. She was checking her inventory when he came down the stairs, opened and closed the door to the apartment, and greeted Chester.

"What are you doing here, boy?" he said.

Ali went to the supply room door and stopped, watching him with her dog. Chester had rolled over on his back, and Jake had complied by rubbing the big shepherd's belly. He was an incredibly handsome man, especially in the morning, she decided. Just looking at him sent her hormones into overdrive.

"Good morning," she said.

He started, looked up at her, then stood. "Morning."

Walking toward him, she smiled. "I thought maybe you'd come up for breakfast this morning. Treat us to pecan pancakes or one of your world-famous omelets."

He looked a bit uncomfortable, which was fine with her. She wanted him a little off balance. "Sorry. I promised Lindsay I'd go out to Lost Springs this morning."

"Really?" Ali took a step closer, determined to close the distance her parents' arrival had put between them. "Why's that?"

"I'm going to talk to some of the boys about wilderness safety."

"That's nice." She reached up and straightened his collar, thinking how good he smelled. Like soap, shampoo and the faintest hint of aftershave. "Are you sure it wasn't because my parents are up there?"

He looked a bit confused. "What?"

"The reason you wouldn't come up to the house this morning," she said. "Are you sure it wasn't because of my parents?"

"Ali…" He shook his head and backed away.

She knew she was more right than wrong and stepped into the space he'd just opened between them. "Jake, my parents are only going to be here for a few days before going back to Atlanta. I probably won't see them again until Christmas."

"What does that have to do with me?"

"Nothing." She tilted her head in a slight shrug.

"Except that I imagine I'll be seeing a lot more of you than that." Again she smiled, knowing she was getting to him when he glanced at her mouth and then quickly looked away. "For Sam's sake, that is."

"I told you I was staying for the summer," he said, his voice a little harsher than normal.

"It *would* be just for Sam's sake, wouldn't it, Jake?" She took another step forward, almost touching him, and sensed his sharp intake of breath.

"Ali, what are you trying to do?"

"Just clarifying things."

"What things?"

In answer, she placed her hands on his shoulders, rose up on her tiptoes and brushed her lips against his. She felt the tension in him as he fought to remain unresponsive. But as she pressed her entire body against his, she also felt him lose the battle. With a deep groan, he brought his arms around her waist, pulled her closer and deepened the kiss. Ali wound her arms around his neck, knowing this was right and wondering how either of them could have ever thought otherwise.

Several fast heartbeats later, Jake broke away from her mouth, but didn't relinquish his hold on her waist. "Damn it, Ali," he said in a hoarse whisper. "What if someone came in?"

"Would that really be so terrible? It was only a kiss." But it felt like more. It felt like victory. "Answer one question for me."

"Ali..." He started to back up, but she kept her arms around his neck.

"One simple question," she insisted. He looked at her warily, and she continued without waiting for his reply. "If you'd known about Sam all those years ago, would you have left me?"

He reached up and removed her arms from around his neck, and this time succeeded in putting distance between them. "I don't want to get into this now."

"I'm not looking for any discussion." She crossed her arms but kept her voice light—as if his answer didn't matter. "Just a simple yes or no will do. I think you owe me that."

He sighed and looked away, clearly uneasy. "No," he finally admitted. "I wouldn't have left if I'd known you were pregnant."

She smiled. In her heart she'd always known it. It had been her logical, practical nature that had doubted him. And herself.

"You believe me?" he asked, looking at her suspiciously. "Just like that."

"Of course." She moved forward, wrapped her arms around his waist and rested her head against his chest. It took him a moment, but finally he enclosed her in his arms. "And remember last weekend," she said. "When I asked you how you felt about me, and you said I was a nice kid?"

She felt rather than saw him nod.

"You never answered my question." She paused, letting doubt stop her temporarily. Then, steeling herself against fear's talons, she said, "Did you love me, Jake?"

He tightened his hold on her and took a deep breath. "Yes. I loved you."

"Good." She lifted her head again, looking into his eyes and smiling an invitation. After a moment's hesitation, Jake accepted, showing her with his mouth what he'd told her in words.

Suddenly, Chester took off barking, startling them apart like guilty teenagers. A moment later there was the crunch of gravel as a car pulled into the yard.

"Are you expecting someone?" Jake asked.

"No." Ali stepped out of his arms and glanced at her watch. "The poodles aren't supposed to be picked up until after twelve. And—"

"Mom!" Sam raced into the kennel. "Mom, it's Brad and his dad."

Surprised, Ali glanced at Jake, who looked equally puzzled. "Got me," he said.

"Come on," Sam insisted as she headed back outside. "They're waiting."

With a shrug, Jake took Ali's arm. "Let's go see what the man wants."

They started for the door, but before going through, Ali stopped.

"Jake, wait."

"What is it?"

"Just this." She rose up on her tiptoes and kissed him again, lightly this time, but with a promise of more to come. "That's just to remind you that we have a conversation to finish."

Smiling to herself, she stepped out into the bright sunshine.

Jake remained for a moment in the dark interior of the kennel, stunned.

No doubt about it, he would never understand women. If he didn't know better, he'd think Ali had come out here this morning with the express purpose of driving him mad. He'd finally decided to keep their relationship platonic, and now she was coming on to him. He didn't have any idea what could have happened between last night and this morning to make her change her attitude about their relationship. Now Ted Gibbons was outside, so he couldn't find out exactly what was going on.

He wondered if she'd planned that, too.

Outside, he found her waiting for him just beyond the door, while Ted Gibbons and her parents stood on the front porch talking. A sleek black limo was parked in the drive, with three men—two bodyguards and a chauffeur, Jake supposed—standing silently beside it. Jake glanced around, looking for Sam and Brad, and saw them in the field behind the house, throwing a ball for Chester. Well, at least the dog was happy about the new arrivals.

"Ready?" she asked, and gave him another of those sexy smiles.

"You're not playing fair, Ali."

"Well, you know what they say about love and war."

"So which circumstance applies to us?"

Laughing, she headed off across the yard toward her guests. "Good morning, Mr. Gibbons," she said brightly. "What an unexpected surprise."

"I'm sorry to barge in on you like this, but—"

"Don't worry about it," Ali assured him. "Would you like to go inside?"

"No, thank you. Brad and I have a plane to catch in Cheyenne." Then, shifting his attention to Jake, he added, "But I wanted to talk to Mr. Merrill before we left."

Jake stepped forward and extended his hand. "It's Jake."

The other man took his hand. "Then you can call me Ted." He looked uncomfortable, glancing from Jake and Ali to the older couple.

"Would you like to go somewhere more private?" Jake offered.

"No, this is fine." He took a deep breath. "I came to thank you for saving my son's life last weekend."

Shoving his hands into his back pockets, Jake said, "That's not necessary. Besides—" he glanced at Sam and Brad, still occupied with Chester "—your son wasn't the only child on that cliff."

"Yes, I know." Gibbons followed Jake's gaze to the children and the dog. "Still, I wanted to let you know how much I appreciate what you did." Turning back to Jake, he reached inside his jacket and pulled a thin envelope from his pocket. "This is for you."

Suddenly uneasy, Jake hesitated.

"Please," Gibbons said.

Jake took the envelope, opened it and pulled out a slim piece of paper. It was a check for more money than Jake made in a year. Hell, it was more than he made in five years. He returned the check to its envelope and held it out to the other man. "I'm sorry, I can't accept this."

Gibbons looked at Jake's outstretched hand but didn't take the check. "Why not?"

"I'm not for sale, Mr. Gibbons."

"I didn't mean it like that."

"Maybe not, but that's how it would feel if I accepted."

Bewilderment shadowed the other man's eyes. "Look, I just wanted to show my appreciation." He glanced behind Jake, evidently looking for support from Ali or her parents.

Jake doubted whether he could explain to a man like Gibbons—a man reported to be one of the wealthiest in the world, who was probably surrounded by people with their hands out—why a lowly Forest Service employee would turn down a small fortune. Instead, he said, "Thank you," dropped the envelope in Gibbons's hand, stepped back and nodded toward the kids. "The lives of those children are all the thanks I need."

Gibbons slipped the envelope back into his suit pocket with an expression that just might have been respect. "If that's the way you feel about it."

Jake remained silent. As far as he was concerned, there was nothing else to say.

"Brad, we've got to go," Gibbons called to the boy. With a nod to Ali and her parents, he said, "It was nice meeting you folks." Then to Jake he added, "If you change your mind—"

"I won't."

Gibbons nodded and smiled. "I imagine you won't."

Sam and Brad ran over to join the adults. Gibbons rested a hand on his son's shoulder, and after saying their goodbyes, the two of them returned to the limousine and drove away.

Jake waited until the sleek vehicle had disappeared before turning to Ali. "I need to get going," he said. "I'm expected out at Lost Springs." He glanced behind her to her parents, who had watched the entire exchange. He couldn't read her mother's expression, but the disapproval on Charles's face was hard to miss. To Sam he said, "Spend the day with your grandparents, and I'll see you when I get back from Lost Springs Ranch."

For once Sam seemed subdued. With a quick nod, she headed back to the porch as Jake started toward his Jeep.

Ali followed.

"Jake," she said as he started to climb in. "Wait."

"I'm late, Ali." Gibbons's visit had left Jake irritable and on edge. This wasn't the time for Ali and him to discuss their on-again, off-again relationship.

"I'm sorry," she said. "For what Ted Gibbons just tried to do."

Jake looked at her and frowned. "Why should you be sorry?"

"I know he insulted you, but I don't think he meant to. Money is all he knows. I think he was honestly trying to thank you."

"That kind of money comes with strings, Ali," he said. "And I won't be Ted Gibbons's puppet. But then, maybe you think I should have taken it. It would have put us on more equal footing."

She looked at him, stunned, and he immediately regretted his sharp words. "I'm sorry, Ali, that was uncalled-for. I'm…" He ran a hand through his hair, glancing again at the threesome on the porch before looking back at Ali. "I need to get going."

With that, he climbed into his Jeep and pulled out of the yard.

Intentionally or not, Ted Gibbons had just reminded Jake of everything he wasn't. Of everything he could never give to Ali and Sam. Of why, as soon as the summer was over, he needed to return to Colorado.

## CHAPTER TWELVE

JAKE NEEDED THE DAY at Lost Springs Ranch.

It gave him time to think and to see things clearly. First, he owed Ali an apology. She'd never once made him feel inadequate because of the difference in their financial situations. It had been his problem and his alone.

Things had seemed so good between them last weekend at her cabin. He'd begun to hope that maybe there could be some future for them—even as he acknowledged the problems that would cause. Since finding Sam, however, Ali had kept her distance, raising a wall between them he wasn't sure he could breach. But he'd been willing to try. For her and their daughter.

Then Ali's parents had shown up, and Jake had realized how inadequate he was for the job of becoming a husband and a father. After all, what did he know about being part of a family? Watching Sam and Ali with her parents made him realize that. So he'd resigned himself to walking away. He'd done it once. He could do it again.

Then she'd shown up in the kennel this morning and turned him around again. Lord knew he wanted her—all of her—body, heart and soul. But having her, well, that was something else entirely. She tempted him to throw caution to the wind and claim her and

Sam as his own, despite his common sense reasons why they weren't good for each other. It left him feeling like he was astride a bucking bronc, and he didn't know whether to let go and brace for the fall, or keep holding on.

Fortunately, working with the boys at the ranch gave him respite.

He'd worked with kids before, giving lectures on wilderness safety to bright, interested faces. The boys at Lost Springs were different. Bright, yes. Interested, some. But also angry and frightened, tough and fragile. Jake felt a kinship with these boys that he'd never experienced with a group of kids before. He understood them, because he'd once been one of them.

Lindsay must have picked up on his connection with her charges. She expressed her gratitude and told Jake she wished he was going to stay in the Lightning Creek area permanently. She would love to set up a regular training course for her boys. She needed someone to teach them respect for the mountains, the way her father had once done.

By the time Jake returned to Ali's late that afternoon, the sun had sunk to the top of the western horizon and dusk was settling in. He pulled into the yard, tired and wanting nothing more than a shower and a few hours of sleep. The last person he wanted to see or speak with was Charles Kendrick, but Ali's father sat alone on the front porch. Jake made a quick survey of the yard, noticing that the big white rental was still there while Ali's car was gone.

Jake climbed out of his Jeep. He considered heading straight for the kennel and the privacy of his apartment but couldn't bring himself to do it. This man had taken care of Ali and Sam when Jake had not, and for that he owed the man something. Respect, if nothing else.

Jake nodded as he approached the porch. "Good evening, Mr. Kendrick."

"If you're looking for my daughter and granddaughter, they went with Margaret into town for dinner."

"You didn't go with them?"

"Nope. I thought I'd hang around here and see if you showed up."

"You have something to say to me?" Jake crossed his arms, bracing himself for the verbal attack he'd known was coming since this man's arrival.

"I thought the two of us could have a little talk without all the female ears around."

"That's fair," Jake said, though the last thing he wanted was to have this or any other conversation with Ali's father.

"I guess I don't have to tell you that I don't like you being here," the older man said without further preamble.

"No, sir. I pretty much figured that one out on my own."

"I don't like it that you think you can waltz back into my daughter's life and pick up where you left off." Charles stood, staring at Jake with hostile eyes. "And I particularly don't like you suddenly taking an interest in my granddaughter."

Jake considered reminding him that Sam was *his* daughter, and that up until a week ago he hadn't known of her existence. But he kept his silence. He understood Charles's need to protect Ali and Sam. *His* family. Not Jake's.

"I don't know why you walked out on my little

girl all those years ago, and I don't care to know. All I know is that you hurt her. You hurt her real bad.''

"I'm sorry for that," Jake said, but offered no further explanation.

"Hah!" Charles stepped closer to the edge of the porch. "I know they keep calling you a hero, but I don't buy it. A man who walks away from a woman the way you did my daughter isn't a hero as far as I'm concerned."

Jake couldn't agree more, but he didn't think Charles would believe him. "What do you want from me, Mr. Kendrick?"

"I want you out of her life. Out of both of their lives."

Jake took a deep breath. He had expected nothing less. "I'm afraid I can't oblige you, Mr. Kendrick. Sam is my daughter, and I plan to be her father. You, of all people, should understand that. As for Ali, well, sir, your daughter is a grown woman. I think what's between us is none of your business."

Charles's eyes blazed furiously. "What do you want, Merrill? Money?"

For the second time in one day someone was trying to buy him off, and it angered Jake. At least Ted Gibbons had offered his check fairly innocently. He couldn't say the same for Charles Kendrick.

Jake met the anger in the other man's eyes with his own. "I suggest we both forget you just said that."

For a moment, neither of them spoke. The silence spun out, heavy and angry between them. Jake could only guess what else Charles would say or offer, because the sound of an approaching car ended their conversation. Jake turned just as Ali pulled into the yard. She and her mother got out, and Ali motioned for Jake to come over to them. He went to the car as she opened the back door. Inside, spread across the back seat, Sam slept.

"She had a very eventful day," Ali said softly. "Think you can carry her in for me?"

Jake reached into the car and lifted the lanky child into his arms. She half woke, saw who held her and smiled. "Hi, Dad."

"Hey, sport," Jake whispered, and tucked her closer in his arms.

Ali shut the car door, and Jake carried Sam up to the house. He paused for a moment on the porch, locking gazes with Charles for a moment, before following Ali inside.

ALI WENT TO LOOK FOR JAKE a half hour later.

She'd known the moment she'd pulled into the yard that her father and Jake had had words. They reminded her of a couple of stallions, facing off over domination of the herd. She wanted to throttle them both right there and then, but knew neither of them would have the faintest idea why. Her father was trying to protect her because he thought he'd failed her twelve years ago. And Jake. Proud, defiant Jake. How she loved him. And she knew he still loved her. Now she had to make sure her father hadn't driven him away.

After putting Sam to bed, she found Jake behind the converted barn, propped against the split-rail fence that separated the yard from the meadow. Next to him, Chester sat as well, staring off in the distance like the man at his side. Not only Sam and Ali but their dog had decided this man belonged here.

Walking up beside him, she leaned against the railing, as well. "Hey," she said.

He glanced down at her. "Hey."

She let the silence stretch out for a bit, studying the landscape, trying to see it as he must. But it was too dark to see anything besides the shadowy line of trees in the distance. Finally, she said, "How did things go at Lost Springs today?"

"Good."

Great. He was into one-word answers. "Are you going to tell me what happened, or make me pull it out of you one word at a time?"

He sighed and turned sideways to look at her. "I spent the day with six different groups of boys. Since Bob Duncan died, they haven't had anyone to teach them wilderness survival. I couldn't do much in the time given, but I answered questions, cleared up some misconceptions and generally got the idea that these kids needed more than I could give them in an hour."

"So...what are you going to do about it?"

He shifted back to stare into the darkness. "I told Lindsay I'd give her a couple of days a week for the rest of the summer. That will leave the rest of the time open to spend with Sam."

Yes, Sam. He was willing to admit to needing Samantha, but what about her? She wanted to hear Jake say he needed to spend time with the mother as well as the daughter.

"There's one other thing," he said. "Lindsay offered to let me stay on at the ranch. She can't afford to pay me, but she can give me room and board."

"What did you tell her?" Alarm nudged its way into Ali's voice.

He studied her for a moment. "I told her I'd think about it."

"You already have a free place to stay." She hadn't meant to blurt it out quite like that, but fear had sharpened her tongue.

"And I'm beginning to wonder if that's such a good idea. I could still—"

"What did my father say to you?"

"He didn't say anything that wasn't true."

"Did he happen to mention that Sam wants you to stay here?" She moved closer and touched his arm. "That *I* want you to stay here."

He shook his head. "Ah, Ali."

"Don't 'Ah, Ali' me." His stubbornness infuriated her, and she pulled her hand away. "You asked me last Sunday, before you went back to Colorado, about us. About where *we* stood. I didn't want to talk about it then. I was frightened. Well, I want to talk about it now. Where do we stand, Jake?"

"There is no 'we,' Ali."

"I don't believe that." Why couldn't he see the obvious? "There's something between us that neither of us can deny. And I'm not sure either of us can walk away from it anymore, either."

"You're wrong. That's exactly what I'm going to do."

It was as if he'd slapped her, and she stepped back. For a long moment, she couldn't speak. Then she rallied. "This is my father's fault."

"No." He shook his head again. "But talking to him, seeing the four of you together, made me realize a few things."

"What things?" she demanded.

"That I don't belong here."

"That's not true," she countered. "You belong to me. And Sam."

"No, Ali..."

"*You're* afraid." The realization struck her, sharp, clear and undeniable. "You're afraid, just like you were twelve years ago, that if you allow yourself to love me, I'll leave you."

"Don't do this, Ali," he warned, his voice laced with sadness.

"Don't try and deny it. It's the truth. Only this time, you're telling yourself it's okay because you're confronting me with it." She grabbed his arm and made him look at her. "But it's not okay. I'm *not* your mother."

"My mother?" Even in the darkness she could see the flash of anger in his eyes. "What does she have to do with this?"

"Your mother left you, just as surely as if she'd packed up and skipped town."

"She never left me," he denied.

"Maybe not physically. But she left a small, frightened boy to his own resources." Ali hesitated, her heart aching for the boy he'd been. For the man he was. Then she pushed on, because she loved him more than she hurt for him. "She left you to find your own way on the street. And you can't forget that."

He turned away, the long lines of his body rigid with tension.

She'd struck a chord. But she wasn't done with him yet. "And what about after you came to Lost Springs? Did she ever once visit you?"

"You think I wanted her to visit me?" He spun on her, his voice harsh and angry. "She was a drunk and a whore. I hated her and never wanted to see her again.''

"That's what you told yourself, and me." Ali softened her voice. "But I never believed it. Somehow you always managed to hang around the ranch on visitors' day."

"No—"

"Oh, you didn't stay in the house like the other boys," Ali continued. "Nothing so obvious. But you were always somewhere they could find you. Just in case."

His jaw tightened.

"And it's the same with this thing you have about reporters," she said, pushing him, willing him to see the truth. "You say you don't like the exposure, that you don't want them making you into a hero when you're only doing your job. But that's not it at all. You're afraid they'll dig too deep, look too closely at Jake Merrill, Mountain Rescue Squad coordinator, and find a frightened little boy."

"That's enough, Ali." This time the warning was hard and angry. "You've gone too far."

But she wasn't afraid of him. Or his anger. "I haven't gone nearly far enough." Besides, her anger matched his. "Damn it, Jake, can't you see what you're doing? I'm *not* your mother. And you're no longer that little boy. I love you and I'm not ever going to leave you."

"This has nothing to do with my mother," Jake said, his rigid control snapping. "So stop trying to psychoanalyze me. Look around you. Look at this place. At that cabin in the Laramie Mountains. What do I have to offer you, Ali? What can I possibly give you that you don't already have or can't get on your

own? And what do I know about families? About
being a father or a husband? Nothing!'' He made a
sweeping gesture with his arm, dismissing the subject
and her. ''Go on, Ali. Go back to your family. You're
better off without me.''

She took a step back and shook her head. ''You're
a fool, Jake Merrill.''

''No, I'm a realist.''

''You've already given me the most important
thing in my life. And you don't even see it.'' She let
her anger loose, let him see how much she cared and
how much he could hurt her. ''You're running away,
just like you did before. Only this time, I'm not going
to let you pretend you're doing it for me.'' She took
a step closer to him. ''Think about that and tell me
I'm wrong. If you can.''

He stared at her in silence, then turned away.

Forcing back her tears, she waited, then backed up.
One step, then two. Still he didn't speak. So she
turned slowly and walked away, angry and hurt, but
refusing to cry. Not now. Not this time. If he didn't
see reason, there would be time later for tears.

Inside the house, she made her excuses to her parents and went to her room. It was a long night with
little sleep. She lay awake for hours, willing Jake to
see reason, to trust her as she'd learned to trust him.

When she awoke the next morning, Jake was gone.

JAKE TOOK OFF for the mountains, driving north this
time toward the Black Hills.

His mind went back over the last month, a time
that had spun his world around and left it in turmoil.
Until the day of the bachelor auction, he'd settled into
his existence, comfortable with his work and his sol-

itude. Then Ali had blown back into his life and shattered his contentment. For three weeks he'd fought against the pull of her, against the need to see her, touch her, love her again. His struggles had come to nothing, because in the end he'd gone to her, to her isolated cabin in the Laramie Mountains, and found the heart he'd lost years ago.

That had been a week ago.

Seven short days that felt at once like an eternity, and at the same time, like the space of several heartbeats. So much had happened. Ali, a beacon calling him toward a light he'd only known with her, had come to love him again. And Sam. He'd found and fallen for the daughter he hadn't even known he had. Then Ali's parents and Ted Gibbons had reminded Jake of everything he would never be.

In the distance, Devil's Tower rose against the backdrop of the Black Hills. The stark monolith of stone stood alone, separate from the mountains that ringed it on two sides. Jake hadn't realized he'd driven so far. Pulling off the road, he found a grassy knoll with a clear view of the tower and parked the Jeep. Settling back against the headrest, he closed his eyes.

Ali had called him a fool. And at the moment he felt like one.

He'd spent twelve years apart from her, living his lonely life. Now she'd offered him everything he'd always wanted. A home. A family. Her. And he'd turned away from her again.

She'd been right.

He *was* running, just as that long-ago boy had once done. And out here, in the shadow of the granite monolith, he could admit it. He was afraid. Afraid that the woman he loved more than life itself would someday wake up and wonder why she'd tied herself to a man like him.

He thought of his mother. She'd been a weak woman. Unable to reconcile herself to his father's desertion, she'd turned to alcohol and other men. In the process she'd destroyed herself and nearly destroyed her son. But Jake had survived. With the help of Bob Duncan, he'd found a place for himself, and in knowing Ali, he'd found hope. But Ali had been right; despite everything his mother had done and hadn't done, Jake had loved her. Until the day she died, he'd never given up on her. Still, despite the care he'd provided once he'd been able, she died a lonely, angry woman. It was time to face the fears she'd instilled in him and put them aside.

All the rest were just excuses.

Ali didn't care that he had nothing material to give her. If she'd been concerned about money, she would have chosen to set up a cushy suburban practice on the outskirts of Atlanta. Instead, she'd returned to Lightning Creek, a speck-of-nothing town in the middle of Wyoming where she probably spent more time in mud and muck than tending people's pets. As for him, he was no longer a rootless boy on the verge of becoming a criminal. He might not have the financial resources of Ted Gibbons, or even Ali's father, but he was far from destitute. He'd found a place for himself in the world and work that meant something.

As for being part of a family, he loved Ali and Sam. Anything else he needed to know, they could teach him.

Twelve years ago, he'd made excuses and paid the price. He'd sacrificed both their happiness to prevent some possible disaster in the future. Now he'd almost done the same thing again. From some people's perspective, he and Ali were a bad match. But they fit together in ways that were more vital than anyone else could see. Together they were complete, and he couldn't let his own foolish pride, or fear, get in the way of that.

He made a few stops on the way back to Lightning Creek. Over the years he'd developed a few connections, people who knew about jobs in the area. So by the time he pulled up to Ali's house, it was late afternoon. The yard was empty, but both cars were sitting out front.

As he climbed out of the Jeep and slammed the door, Chester and Sam came running from the back of the house.

"Dad," she called. "I told them you'd be here soon." She jumped into his arms and he held her as if his life depended on it.

"Come on," she said, squirming out of his embrace. "Grandpa's grilling steaks and they're almost ready."

Holding his daughter's hand, Jake circled the house to the backyard. Charles Kendrick stood over the barbecue grill, and Margaret was setting the table.

"Oh, you're just in time," Margaret said with a smile that outshone her husband's frown. "Go on and get cleaned up."

Just then, Ali pushed through the screen door, holding a pitcher of iced tea. She stopped. "Jake?"

Ali had heard the slamming of the car door in front, Chester's excited bark, and Sam's squeal of welcome. But she hadn't let herself believe he'd come back. Nor would she jump to conclusions now. He'd said he was going to stay for the summer because of Sam. That could be why he was here now. To see his daughter.

Releasing Sam's hand, Jake took a step toward her. "Hey," he said. "I hear we're having steaks for dinner."

"You're back." *Great,* she thought. *You sound like the village idiot.*

He smiled, that heart-stopping smile that always took her breath away, and moved closer. Taking the pitcher from her hand, he set it on the picnic table. "Yes, I'm back."

"For how long?" She was afraid to ask but she had to know.

Jake reached into his pocket and pulled out a small black velvet box. "For as long as you'll have me."

Ali's hands trembled as she reached for the box. She wouldn't let herself believe it. Not yet.

"What is it?" Sam asked, coming up beside her.

Margaret intercepted the curious eleven-year-old. "Hush, dear."

Ali opened the box and tears filled her eyes. Inside, a pear-shaped ruby nestled against black satin.

"It reminded me of a teardrop," he said. She looked up at him and he added, "For the years we spent apart, and the love that drew us back together."

Ali couldn't speak, couldn't move, and she saw the momentary fear flicker in his eyes.

"I want to marry you, Ali." Jake stepped forward and took her hand. "I don't have much, but I love you. I love you both."

In answer, she threw her arms around his neck, still unable to speak as the tears streamed down her face. A moment later, she felt Sam's small arms snake around her waist, and both she and Jake reached down to include the child.

And Ali knew, she'd finally succeeded in reclaiming Jake.

# EPILOGUE

*Two months later*

"COME ON, DAD, WAKE UP. We have a surprise for you."

Jake opened his eyes and groaned. "What? Where's your mother?"

"In the kitchen making breakfast."

"What time is it?" Jake looked at the bedside clock with its bright digital numbers. It wasn't even six yet.

"The sun's up," Sam said, as if reading his mind.

Jake glanced at the gray light in the window. "Barely."

"Come on. You've got to get up. We have to be there by nine. And we need to take care of the animals before we go. And eat breakfast. And get cleaned up. And—"

"Whoa," Jake said, trying to slow her down. "Okay, I'll get up. But where do we have to be by nine?" He'd managed to get a partial transfer from the Forest Service. He worked two-week rotations, dividing his time between Colorado and Wyoming. And unless he was remembering wrong, this was his weekend off.

Sam shook her head. "I can't tell you. It's a surprise and Mom will kill me if I spoil it." She bounced off the bed and headed for the door, stopping before going out. "Now, don't make me have to come in here again."

Jake groaned and thought he just might move back out to the loft apartment and change all the locks. But what was the point? He had no doubt Sam would find a way in.

By the time he got showered and dressed, Ali and Sam were already down at the kennel taking care of the animals. Ali had left a bagel in the toaster oven and a pot of coffee. He wanted a real breakfast, but evidently, whatever his two women had cooked up for him didn't include food.

Sam came back first, but before he could get a word out of her, she disappeared into her bedroom. Shades of things to come, Jake thought. Another two years and she'd be a bona fide teenager, spending all her time behind closed doors. Thinking of Sam entering adolescence made him think of Charles Kendrick. Although he hadn't been thrilled that Ali and Jake had decided to marry, in the end he'd come around. Not that he'd ever hold any affection for his son-in-law, but he accepted him. Jake could only hope he could be as tolerant of the man who would someday enter his daughter's life.

Ali returned about a half hour later, and like her daughter, she avoided him easily by claiming she didn't have much time.

As he heard the shower turn on, he settled into a kitchen chair with Chester at his feet. "Well, buddy," Jake said. "How about if *you* tell me what's going on?"

The dog yawned, thumped his tail on the floor and lowered his head to his paws.

"Looks like you're in cahoots with the women. I'll remember that."

A few minutes later, Ali came back into the kitchen, dressed in the same simple dress she'd worn the day of the Lost Springs bachelor auction. She looked as fresh and sweet as the peachy color of her dress, and Jake pulled her into his arms before she could voice another protest. She tasted as good as she looked. Two months of marriage, and he still hadn't gotten enough of her. As he'd told her that first night in her cabin, he doubted whether he ever would.

She broke the kiss all too soon. "Not now, or we'll be late."

"Okay," he said. "Now you've really got my attention. Where exactly are we going?"

Ali placed her hands on his shoulders and kissed him again lightly before stepping out of his arms. "Go put on your suit."

"My suit?" He'd bought it for the wedding and figured he wouldn't have to put it on again for some time. Maybe not until Samantha got married.

"You heard me," she said. "And hurry. It's hanging on the back of the door and there's a shirt there, as well."

"Ali…"

"Do it for me. Please." She gave him a secret smile that promised all sorts of wicked pleasures. "You won't be disappointed."

Of course, he couldn't say no, so he headed for the bedroom, stopping only when Sam—no, Samantha—came out of her room.

He let out a low wolf whistle. "Well, well," he said. "Don't you look pretty."

She rolled her eyes and stomped past him. He

guessed a man wasn't supposed to notice the first time his eleven-year-old tomboy put on a dress. Or even mention that she looked pretty. Well, if Sam could wear a dress, he could put on his suit.

A few minutes later he joined them in the kitchen. "Okay," he said. "What's next?"

Sam and Ali exchanged a smile, then Sam produced a white handkerchief. "For your eyes," she said.

With hands held up in front of him, he backed up. "Don't you think this is carrying things a little too far?"

"Dad, you're going to ruin it."

Of course he gave in. He had no defense against the two of them when they sided together. He let Sam blindfold him and Ali lead him to the car. It wasn't a long drive—wherever they were taking him. Several times Jake was tempted to peek out from under the cloth, but he had a feeling his daughter was watching him like a hawk.

When the car pulled to a stop and Ali shut off the engine, Sam said, "Okay, Dad, you can take off the blindfold now."

Jake slipped the fabric off his eyes and looked around. Lost Springs Ranch. He glanced at Ali, but before he could ask, she said, "You'll see. Come on."

As he climbed out of the car, he noticed they weren't the only ones here this morning. Several other vehicles were parked in front of the house, and about a dozen people milled around on the porch. Jake recognized Lindsay Duncan and Rex Trowbridge, plus the two older women Jake had first seen at the bachelor auction. Sugar Spinelli, who'd bought Rob Carter at the auction for Twyla McCabe, and Theda Duck-worth, Sugar's best friend. Ali's friend Gail and her husband, John, were there, as well, and several other couples whom Jake didn't know.

Lindsay greeted them as they approached the porch. "I'm really glad you could make it. This is a big day."

"Well, if I knew why I was here," Jake grumbled, "or what was going on, I might be glad as well."

Lindsay threw Ali a conspiratorial smile. "All in good time, Jake."

The sound of more approaching vehicles caught their attention. Coming up the road was a string of media vans and trucks. In the lead was the beat-up pickup belonging to the local radio station, followed by a half-dozen others from radio and television stations from as far away as Cheyenne.

Jake instantly tensed, and Ali laid her hand on his arm. "Don't worry," she whispered. "They're not here for you."

He felt instantly foolish, as if every time he saw a reporter they might want to interview him. "Hey," he said with a smile. "I've decided I like reporters."

The vehicles pulled into the yard, and for the next few minutes the news people were busy setting up equipment, asking Lindsay and Rex questions and generally scurrying around. Then someone yelled, "Here he comes."

A long black limousine, led and followed by four black sedans, drove up the road toward the ranch. Reporters hurried to get in position, and Lindsay and Rex stepped to the forefront of onlookers on the porch. "Okay," Lindsay said to the group. "I think we're ready to get started now."

ousine stopped and men poured from the sedans, taking up positions around the larger vehicle. Only then did the limo driver get out and circle around to the back door. He opened it, and Ted Gibbons stepped out. The reporters crowded around him, but his men kept them at bay while Gibbons walked unhindered to the front porch where Lindsay and Rex waited.

"Ms. Duncan, Mr. Trowbridge." He shook their hands. "I'm glad to finally meet both of you in person."

"The pleasure is ours, Mr. Gibbons," Lindsay said. "We can't thank you enough for what you're about to do."

Gibbons smiled and turned on the top step to face the camera. "Are we ready?" he asked the reporters.

"Five seconds, Mr. Gibbons." And the man counted down with his finger. "You're on."

Gibbons fell into an easy television persona, smiling and confident as if he did this every day. "Hello," he started. "I'm Ted Gibbons, president and CEO of Millennium Corporation." He paused, giving his audience time to catch up with him. "As many of you know," he continued, "two months ago my son and two other children were lost in the Laramie Mountains. They spent one full night and most of the next day trapped at the bottom of a mountain crevice. My son, who suffered a slight concussion, was unconscious for most of that time, and one of the other children sprained his ankle. All three were trapped with no way out. They could have all perished."

He took a deep breath and continued, donning just the right tone of solemnity. "Thanks to the efforts of a mountain rescue team, all three children were carried off the mountain safely. But before the team could reach them, a man climbed down into that crevice in the middle of a violent thunderstorm to try and keep those children alive. He brought them food and blankets, but mostly, he brought them hope.''

He paused again, glancing from one expectant face to the other. ''And that's why I'm here today, to bring *hope* to another group of children.

''Lost Springs Ranch has been working wonders for troubled boys for over fifty years. All anyone has to do is look at their track record. Among the ranch's alumni are doctors, lawyers, successful businessmen, and the man who climbed into that mountain crevice to give three scared and frightened children hope. The man who saved my son's life.''

There was a general murmur from the crowd.

''This man would prefer not to be named,'' Gibbons said. ''And I plan to honor that. But I also want to recognize the people and the place that helped make him the man he is—Lost Springs Ranch.'' Gibbons paused again, his timing perfect and dramatic. ''But this isn't about just one man, it's about all the boys who once lived here and grew into responsible adults. And it's about the boys who live here now, and who will live here in the future. And it's about the fine men and women who spend their lives teaching these boys.'' He looked at Lindsay and lifted a hand. ''Ms. Duncan.''

Lindsay stepped up beside Gibbons. ''Ms. Duncan, on behalf of my son and myself, I have set up an endowment for Lost Springs Ranch. My company, Millennium Corporation, has ceded five million dollars to the endowment. I personally have added another million. Also, I have established a small department within my company to monitor and raise more funds for Lost Springs Ranch. They will approach other large corporations looking for humanitarian causes.''

Huge applause broke out, but Gibbons held up his hand to silence it. ''With this fund,'' he said, ''you should be able to continue your excellent work here at Lost Springs Ranch for many years to come.''

With tears in her eyes, Lindsay spoke into the microphone. ''Thank you, Mr. Gibbons. From all our boys. Past. Present. And future.''

After that there was a flurry of questions and answers. Jake and Ali melted to the back of the crowd. They didn't speak. There didn't seem to be much to say in the face of this kind of generosity. After a few minutes, Ted Gibbons turned and searched out Jake. With his men at his side, he pushed through the crowd and offered Jake his hand. ''I hope this meets with your approval, Mr. Merrill.''

Jake took the other man's hand. ''You've done a good thing here.''

Gibbons smiled broadly. ''Thank you.'' With his men once again flanking him, he returned to the waiting limousine, taking the reporters and cameras with him.

''You know, I sure could use someone who understands wilderness survival. I could even afford to pay that person now.''

Jake turned to Lindsay, who had come up beside them unnoticed.

''The boys need someone like you,'' she said. ''Someone who really understands the wild country. And who understands them. What do you say? Can you give me a couple of days a month?''

Jake slipped his arms around his wife's shoulders

and looked at her. "What do you say, Ali? Think I should take it?"

"I think you should do what you want. But you've got a real talent with kids. It would be a shame to waste it."

Lowering his head, he kissed her, wondering what he'd ever done to deserve this woman.

"Come on, you guys," Sam said, obviously embarrassed. "Not here."

Laughing, Jake stepped away from Ali and reached for his daughter. Sam squealed but didn't fight too hard as he gave her a bear hug "So, what do you think, sport? Think your dad should spend his days with a bunch of rowdy boys?"

"As long as you're *my* dad, it's okay by me."

Jake hugged her again, then reached for her mother and wrapped her in his other arm. "You can count on that."

Over their shoulders he saw Lindsay smiling at the three of them. "I take it that's a yes," she said.

"You bet," Jake answered. "Only I won't take your money."

"But—" Lindsay started to object.

"Consider it payback for all Lost Springs did for me," Jake said. "That's my proposition. Take it or leave it."

"Well," Lindsay said. "Looks like I don't have much choice. I'll take it." She smiled broadly and added, "Thanks." Then she returned to the milling crowd that was still buzzing after Ted Gibbons's announcement.

"So, what do you really think?" Jake asked Ali.

She answered him with a kiss and Jake knew he'd

found his true place in the world. He'd found work where he could make a difference. He'd discovered a daughter he adored. And he'd reclaimed a woman, his wife, who made all the rest that much sweeter.

# FREE BOOK OFFER!

In August, an exciting new
*Maitland Maternity* single title comes
with a FREE BOOK attached to it!

## by Marie Ferrarella

This brand-new single title revisits all the
excitement and characters that you've enjoyed in
the *Maitland Maternity* continuity series—but there's
more! As part of this extraordinary offer, the first
title in Harlequin's new *Trueblood, Texas* continuity
will be shrink-wrapped to the *Maitland Maternity* book
absolutely FREE! An amazing "2-for-1" value that
will introduce you to the wonderful
adventure and romance of

## TRUEBLOOD, TEXAS

*On sale in August 2001 at your favorite retail outlet.*

**HARLEQUIN®**
*Makes any time special* ®

Presenting three tales by bestselling author

# VICKI LEWIS THOMPSON

## URBAN *Cowboys*

### Cowboy #1: **THE TRAILBLAZER**

Businessman T. R. McGuiness thought ranching would be a breeze—
until sexy cowgirl Freddy Singleton showed him how
much more he had to learn....

### Cowboy #2: **THE DRIFTER**

Trucker Chase Lavette was looking forward to having time alone
on the range—until his former lover showed up with
a little surprise....

### Cowboy #3: **THE LAWMAN**

Cop Joe Gilardini had decided to give up law enforcement—
until mysterious "accidents" started occurring at the ranch...
and he found himself falling for his primary suspect.

**Coming August 2001**

*Every woman loves a cowboy...*

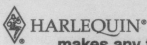